The Meaning of
Consuelo

The Meaning of
Consuelo

JUDITH ORTIZ COFER

BEACON
150

BEACON PRESS
BOSTON

Beacon Press
25 Beacon Street
Boston, Massachusetts 02108-2892
www.beacon.org

Beacon Press books
are published under the auspices of
the Unitarian Universalist Association of Congregations.

Text design by Charlotte Strick

First paperback edition published by Beacon Press in 2004.

09 08 07 06 05 04 8 7 6 5 4 3 2 1

This book is printed on acid-free paper that meets
the uncoated paper ANSI/NISO specifications
for permanence as revised in 1992.

"Witness" from The Rain in the Trees by W. S. Merwin, copyright © 1988
by W. S. Merwin. Used by permission of Alfred A. Knopf,
a division of Random House, Inc.

Library of Congress Cataloging-in-Publication Data
Ortiz Cofer, Judith, 1952–
    The meaning of Consuelo / Judith Ortiz Cofer.— 1st ed.
        p.   cm.
    ISBN 0-8070-8387-9 (pbk.)
    1. Puerto Rico—Fiction.   2. Loss (Psychology)—Fiction.   I. Title.

    PS3565.R7737M43 2003
    813'.54—dc21

                                                      2003004006

This book is for John and Tanya

I want to tell what the forests
were like

I will have to speak
in a forgotten language

—W. S. Merwin,
"Witness"

CONTENTS

The Meaning of
Consuelo

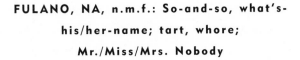

FULANO, NA, n.m.f.: So-and-so, what's-his/her-name; tart, whore; Mr./Miss/Mrs. Nobody

María Sereno walked in his leisurely way toward the cart selling *piragüas* that appeared on our street corner every day at noon. The *fulano* of our neighborhood, María Sereno, born Mario Manuel Santiago Sereno, wore tight red pedal pushers and a man's T-shirt over an obviously empty brassiere. His image contains my earliest understanding of a key phrase in my family's conversations: *el fulano* or *la fulana*; used to refer to the outsider, he or she never called by name.

The flip-flops on his big feet made a slapping beat to the subtle back-and-forth swaying of his hips. His black hair was slicked behind his ears, a coquettish curl wrapped around an earlobe. The women hanging clothes in their backyards or taking a break on their porch rockers stared unashamedly at María, smiling in a superior way or raising an eyebrow at one another. The *piragüero*, seller of ices, was a war veteran with a metal leg. He would sometimes let out a long wolf-whistle as he watched María approach. María Sereno just kept walking regally toward his daily treat of a shaved-ice cone topped with thick, sweet tamarind-and-strawberry syrup, which he would noisily suck on while standing there in front of man, woman, and God. He'd lick it with his long pink tongue. His eyes would be closed in some kind of sugar ecstasy, and then he'd smile enigmatically at no one in particular—like a Puerto Rican Mona Lisa—and head back to his mother's house, where he lived in a room with its own private entrance.

His mother was a widow on a pension and María Sereno was her only child. At the age of twenty-eight, he was still her dependent, since the farthest he would go toward male attire was pedal-pusher pants, which kept him from finding a decent job; any man who hired him would be exposed to ridicule too. He did manage to bring in a little money as a manicurist—a trade at which he excelled. He attended to the hands of women in their own homes, but community rules were strict; María Sereno could never be found in one of our *casas decentes* by a husband or any other adult male; instead he had to knock by prearrangement at the back door and be willing to fall into deception should one of the men arrive unexpectedly. "He came begging for my old nail polish again, the *sinvergüenza*," the woman could then say, shaking her head in amused dismay at the disapproving husband or son. "You know how *they* are. Next he'll want to exchange recipes." And María Sereno would hang his head like a reprimanded child and slink away. That was the deal.

When there were no interruptions by the man of the house, María Sereno would arrange his tools over a black velvet cloth on someone's kitchen table and begin concentrating on the hands of the day. He took pride in his work. My mother was a regular customer, though my sister and I were sworn to secrecy about María Sereno's monthly visits to my mother's kitchen. It was up to me as the oldest to keep Mili, who was only four, from telling. Mili liked

María Sereno. She had confessed to me that she wanted to be a nail-painter like him when she grew up.

In public we were to pretend that we didn't know him. But Mili sometimes forgot. That sunny autumn afternoon, Mili and I tossed a rubber ball back and forth across the little square of yard in front of our new, modern cement house that sat on a street planned according to the geometric designs of North American developers. Our yard was precisely the same size and shape as our neighbors' yards, although there were still, as I quickly learned, subtle indicators of privilege. For example, the well-tended roses, the pruned hibiscus hedges of legitimate house owners were missing from our leased space. Our father was a veteran, and we had earned our suburban life, though we did not own our house. My mother did not see any need to tend a garden on land that did not belong to her. Our barren plot let everyone know that we were not setting roots in this place. Therefore, they were hardly obligated to include us in their communal lives. So, it was as a kind of outsider myself that I began to watch the little dramas of the street and learn the language I'd need for the roles that I was soon to play.

From early on I saw María Sereno go through his daily show of defiance, and the women practice their front-yard deceit. Only eight, I did not know duplicity from manners. It was all what you were told to do, what you had to do to be *gente decente*, decent people, which is what we all thought we were or wanted to be—except for María Sereno.

María Sereno strolled past our yard just as Mili missed catching the ball. He stopped in his tracks, hands on hips, and watched us, apparently fascinated with the pink-and-yellow sphere rolling toward him. Then he looked at Mili and raised one of his heavily drawn arched eyebrows—like those of American movie stars—and opened his mouth in mock horror. Mili giggled, apparently as delighted as I was by María Sereno's ability to transform himself from man to woman, the ultimate clown's trick. I caught my breath as I saw him grab the ball with his free hand—he was still holding the snow cone in the other—and take a few steps into our territory.

I knew I was to yell for Mami if anyone violated our family borders in this American-style neighborhood of strangers—thrown together by circumstance rather than by fate or birth—so unlike her *pueblo* where families and friends lived next to one another. But I froze. Was he friend or foe? He came inside our home often by invitation, though only through the back door. My mother put her beautiful hands into his big ones like she did with Papi—the only two men she touched that way. I stood there frozen in my indecision as María Sereno knelt in front of my little sister, handed her the ball, and, taking her grimy little hand in his, pronounced her nails "*Un desastre, mi amor.*"

Should I have screamed then? We were not to let any man who wasn't in our immediate family of father, grandfathers, and uncles touch us. Women we knew were allowed to caress and kiss us— somehow that was different. But was María Sereno a man or a woman? I could not tell in the bright sunshine of that tropical afternoon. My mother kept saying he had been born a boy. But that was years ago, long before my time. Had he turned into a woman after that?

In total confusion—knowing that we were being spied upon by many eyes up and down our street, by women who would tell Mami that I had let him/her come into our yard and not yelled for her like I had been told to—I turned and dragged Mili kicking and screaming into the house. Gasping, I pushed her toward our mother, who had been mopping the pink tile floor, one of her favorite activities. She mopped daily until she could see her own reflection on the squares imported from Cuba, where Fidel Castro was hiding in the mountains and biding his time before he freed our sister island from its corrupt dictator. She seemed lost in thought, probably daydreaming about that rebel leader whom I had heard her call handsome and *muy macho*, but now, startled, she let the mop drop. Mili grabbed her waist, screaming that I had hurt her. I was glued to the window facing our yard. I saw that María Sereno had dropped his snow cone on the gravel and was picking up the paper cup. I saw the *piragüero*'s face contorted with laughter, saying things I could not hear. He was slapping his metal leg as he looked this way and that, like he was a ringmaster in a circus making certain both sides of the audience had gotten the clown's joke. María crushed the paper cup and stood up. I could feel my mother close behind me with Mili still wrapped around her middle. María rolled the cup around in his palms like I did when playing with dough, then, glancing to both sides of the street as the *piragüero* had done, he reached his hand under his T-shirt and stuffed the paper ball inside it. The result was that he looked like he had grown a lumpy little breast, just one. He then began to walk in the slow regal pace that had been interrupted by our game, and headed toward his mother's house at the end of the street.

My mother watched him too. Her quick breathing told me she was gathering her anger; she reminded me of the new vacuum cleaner Papi had recently bought from a door-to-door salesman. It had been a strange purchase made by a man who did not realize that it's neither easy nor necessary to vacuum ceramic tiles, but who was anxious to provide his family with all the latest amenities of city life. He had been too proud to return the purchase and, in the process, to admit his ignorance to another man, who probably knew exactly what he was doing to this poor *jibaro*.

Mami used the vacuum cleaner on a small rectangular hooked rug just so she could vacuum something and please Papi. The machine always threatened to swallow Mami's little rug in one breath. And that's how Mami seemed to me right then, sucking in her fury, about to blow up. She carried Mili and dragged me into the kitchen.

"Sit down, *niña.*" She ordered me into one of the plastic-covered green metal chairs. All the women we knew had bought them at the Sears store that had just opened in Hato Rey. I sat down and folded my hands on top of the matching green Formica table. I had learned that a submissive posture in the face of parental fury always helped. I started hiccuping a little in preparation for full-fledged sobbing if necessary. I wanted to preserve the tender skin of my calves, which had only recently felt the sting of her new plastic flyswatter, also bought at Sears, a tool she never used on the island's insects, only on her daughter's legs. Mili was staring at me in horror. I knew she had not meant to betray me quite to this extent. El Matamoscas, the evil flyswatter, was about to go after her only sister, her major source of amusement. She started making distress noises too.

But Mami was not going to let our despair spoil her demonstration.

"*Silencio,* both of you." She grabbed the rubber ball, which Mili had been holding like a life preserver to her chest, and, using only her fingertips as if it were covered with slime, Mami dropped it into her shiny aluminum sink, opening the faucet full blast on it. Then she poured disinfecting pine floor cleaner over it. Mili squirmed in her chair, perhaps thinking that Mami intended to do the same to her. My sister was filthy as usual, since she liked playing with the chameleons in our backyard, building modern American-style communities for them out of mud and gravel. Mami sometimes picked her up for a bath with the same expression of disgust on her face as she'd had in handling the ball.

"Now I'm going to tell you this, both of you, but it's up to you, niña, as the oldest, to make sure you don't forget my warning. You are not to talk to that man in public again."

"But Mami . . ." I couldn't help myself. As usual, when I heard a contradiction spoken by an adult, I felt the urge to point out the truth: that Mariá Sereno was not a stranger to us. "He does your nails . . . he's your friend . . ."

"How dare you talk back to me, niña? You are an *entrometida* and a *malcriada*. Now come here, both of you."

I knew those two words. They were used mainly to indict your own children. The first one meant that even if what I had pointed out was *la pura verdad*, like we were always supposed to tell our parents, I was still trespassing into adult territory by bringing it up; being a *malcriada* was even worse. It literally meant that I had not learned better from her; it was an admission of total disappointment in my upbringing. I shuffled over to the sink like a beaten-down prisoner of war, slapping the tile with my flip-flops. Unfortunately, I was wearing nothing but a sundress, which left my skinny legs totally exposed to the bite of the dreaded flyswatter. Mili was now gripped by fear—trembling and uttering choked little sobs. But all Mami did was yank our hands under the stream of lukewarm water and scrub them with *Palmolivé* soap, which killed almost all germs and bacteria, according to the advertisements in her women's magazines. *Palmolivé* soap and Jergens hand cream— the preferred hygienic combination of her house, used both for health and for beauty.

Mami had been seduced by the first advertisements she had seen on television and had remained loyal to the products in the same way her *mamá* professed blind faith in the power of her herbal medicines, disdaining anything that came in a sealed jar. Mami had a less decipherable list of set-in-stone rules about people and relationships that Mili and I were to internalize without question. After we grew up and got married, she assured us, we could make our own rules for our own *casas y familias*. Until then, she spoke like the Pope, with infallibility. "You never know what you can catch from people like that," she would say. Then she'd send us in to take a shower together. We'd be made to stay indoors the rest of the beautiful sunny day, and play in our room with the Venetian blinds drawn shut to remind us of our lowly status as disobedient children, and of our total dependence on her. Mami was the keeper of the keys to our freedom. To her we owed every privilege, even that of playing in the sun.

That day was no different. "We do not associate in public with people like María Sereno," she announced as she sent us to our room.

All afternoon Mili made herself costumes from assorted pieces of our wardrobe—attempting to transform herself into a little María Sereno, stuffing a scarf with socks and tying it around her flat chest, and insisting on painting her nails with the watercolors we were not supposed to play with except under our mother's supervision. Nothing I said made any difference to my sister, who had a way of turning herself into a self-contained, fully automated doll when she wanted to, as unresponsive to others as any stuffed bear on our bed, but manic about the details of her fantasies. Her staged one-girl plays were elaborate—the only element she didn't care about was an audience. These were *her* fantasies, and she didn't need anyone else to enjoy them. Mostly I picked up after her to keep us both out of trouble. There was no way for any of us to know that Mili's talent for losing herself—as if inside her there was a hole she dove into, like Alice in Wonderland—was also the start of our family's spiraling toward what we would always call *la tragedia*, the events leading to the terrible day that changed everything for each of us, forever.

The next time María Sereno did my mother's nails, I sneaked into the kitchen by sliding in with my back close to the wall like a lizard, ready to scramble at the slightest hint of disapproval. But Mami was always in a good mood when she was getting a manicure. She ordered me, without looking, to get María Sereno a glass of ice water. That meant I had to get the plastic glass with the tiny black dot on the bottom down from the closet shelf. It was the one she had marked for his use only. It was kept with the plate and utensils she used when she fed the toothless, smelly old man who came around every few weeks collecting discarded clothing and any piece of junk we wanted to get rid of. She would give him a reheated meal in his special black-dotted dish, and he would eat in the shade of the breadfruit tree in our backyard.

I took the metal ice trays out of the freezer of our new Frigidaire. I ran water on the bottom to loosen the cubes, then, using all my strength, I pulled up the bar that released the perfect little squares of ice. I filled María Sereno's special glass with water from the faucet and placed it in front of him with my eyes averted. I saw that he held my mother's ring finger, the one with her wedding band on it, and he was carefully painting the nail red, like the hibiscus that grew everywhere on our street—the deep blood-red of the flowers clashing with the pastel paint of the cement houses. I sensed his eyes on me, and glanced quickly back at him and then away, feeling inexplicably like crying. María Sereno had looked at me—not in any of the ways I was used to grown-ups assessing me, with affection or disapproval, but in a new way with a different message, one that I was too young to understand but not too young to recognize. It said "betrayal." It said *la traición*. It told me I had somehow caused him pain, but I didn't know exactly how. And maybe it asked me if I thought it couldn't happen to me—if I thought I could never become *la fulana* myself.

MUJER/HOMBRE: Some Early Words

My island is so small it disappears on a globe or a map of the world. But as a child I could not see the end of the land from anywhere I stood, so to me it was as large as I needed my world to be. I was the daughter of a proud and troubled young man and a pretty, vivacious young woman who took pleasure in their children, but I was a *niña seria* from the start, preferring a picture book to the rowdy company of other children, story time to parties. Just like my silent, brooding father. His silences were the vacuum Mami abhorred, having grown up around laughter, shouts, and angry cries—noise meant life for her. I perceived her disappointment and retreated further inward as a result. After my sister, María Milagros, was born when I was four, Mami finally had the cheery companion she thought a child should be.

No one had any doubts as to whom Mili resembled in personality. Even before she had acquired the singular gush of joy that was her greeting to any given day, her dimpled chubby face announced that a ray of tropical sunshine had entered our *casa*. And so we were both to grow into what was predicted for us: the dark sister and the light sister. I was expected to live up to my name, Consuelo, from the word meaning comfort and consolation; Mili, from the word *milagros*, a miracle, was supposed to bring the light into our lives. I was to console, care for, and watch over her.

We hadn't always lived in the capital city; we had moved there the year I started second grade. San Juan was where my father's older brother, a widower, lived with his son, Patricio. Tío Domingo had found my father a job as a maintenance engineer in an American hotel. He also rented us the house next door to his, one of several he owned in a well-kept modern subdivision, still called a *barrio* then, on the outskirts of the spreading capital.

Mami had been reluctant to leave her pueblo on the opposite coast of the island, where her parents and many brothers and sisters were a solace to her during Papi's years as a *mujeriego*, a skirt-chaser. But she also knew that the only way to get him away from the women, particularly one pretty divorcée who paraded herself blatantly in front of our house, was to put some distance between them and him. Even her mother said to her, "*Hija*, this woman is a spider and she is extending her web. It is your duty to get him far away from her grasp." And so we made the trip across the island, around the mountains of the Cordillera Central, and toward the land's end of San Juan where, if you wanted to move forward, you had no choice but to board a ship or an airplane to New York.

That first year in our new home I helped Mami with Mili. I took my role as guardian of my impulsive baby sister so seriously that I began to bite my nails and suffer from mysterious headaches. The doctor told my mother that I needed to get out of my room and act more like an eight-year-old niña instead of an overzealous nanny. My twelve-year-old cousin, Patricio Signe, offered to entertain me some afternoons. He too was an odd child and, like me, a lover of books. He had a special talent for puppet-making, creating elaborate miniature people out of papier-mâché; he dressed them in the bright remnants of fabric he begged from my mother, who had begun altering dresses for the tourist ladies at the Golden Palms Hotel, where Papi worked. Although she was puzzled, as she put it, "by a nearly grown *muchacho* playing dolls" with me, she was glad I was being sociable and sent Patricio bags full of ribbons and patches of expensive material with which to dress our growing cast of puppet people.

Tío Domingo had channeled all his grief over his wife's death into business ventures. She had died in a car accident that had also taken the lives of two other women, all heading for work in the hotels of San Juan's Condado district. Luckily, she had taught their son to take care of himself, so all Tío Domingo had to do was check on Patricio occasionally and make sure he was going to school. The boy even cooked for himself, though Domingo had hired a woman to come in and clean house once in a while, and she sometimes offered to make a home-cooked meal for the poor orphan. The boy's reclusiveness disturbed my uncle. Patricio was too quiet and never brought other boys his age home with him from school. But Patricio was an *hombrecito*, which meant that he didn't have to be watched over or worried about like a niña, and Domingo eventually decided that Patricio would get over his shyness.

Once, Patricio made a *papá* puppet shaped like his father, complete with a papier-mâché beer belly, black hair greased into a pompadour, and a mustache that looked like a paintbrush. I helped him shellac some fake fur from a lady's boa onto a finely sculpted head of plaster painted light brown. The doll's eyeballs were painted all the way to the left, so that even when he faced another puppet, he was looking at the wall. Patricio invented a script for the papá puppet, and it was always a monologue: "*Hola*, Patricio, what are you doing?" Silence. "How is school?" Silence. "Don't you have any friends?" Silence. "*Bueno*, let me know if you need anything. Don't expect me home early tonight." Then, staring away from the invisible son in front of him, the papá puppet would pat the air in a distracted way and walk into several walls before exiting the cardboard stage. It was not the best show we put on, but Patricio insisted on taking out the papá puppet and having a one-sided conversation quite often.

I was always glad when we did the Golden Palms *turista* play. Then Patricio would assign me parts, usually of various rich American ladies speaking broken Spanish to the Puerto Rican hotel staff, all played by him. We had a maid doll, a custodian doll who resembled Papi, and other support players who often pretended not to understand the turistas. The conflict would peak as the turista puppets became more and more frantic and their Spanish more broken, until, finally, the manager puppet came on in his green velvet suit, wearing his painted-on face-wide smile, to mediate. We took our scenarios from what we heard the adults around us describe, and we shrank their concerns and their anger down to twelve-inch size, playing it back for our amusement.

Patricio hardly ever spoke to me in his own voice in those early days, preferring to take on a "character" even when we were just sitting around planning our next creation. Sometimes he would wear a mask made of feathers—taken from a dead seagull he had found on the beach—he called it his *cisne*, or swan mask, a pun on his last name, Signe. The swan was always mute. On those days no words were allowed. We pantomimed everything.

One day, when my mother had taken Mili to the hotel with her to pick up more dresses to hem and alter, I sat with Patricio Signe on the cool tiles of his front porch teaching him some new tricks with my jacks. It was that day that he came up with the idea—my mother would later call it blasphemy—that it is possible to change the natural world. He had been staring at the unusual white hibiscus that his mother had cultivated. My uncle couldn't care less about a yard. I had heard my mother say that he had even joked that he'd like to have concrete poured over it so he could park his cars and work on them. But Patricio cultivated his mother's garden. He examined the leaves and petals under his microscope and conducted experiments in the bathroom with them. I had never been allowed to participate in this part of Patricio's mysterious private life.

Later that day I opened the screen door at the back of Tío Domingo's house—another progressive American idea, keeping the bugs out of your house—to find Patricio holding a real syringe in his gloved hands. He was hunched over vials at the kitchen table, each containing a different color of liquid, concentrating so hard that he didn't even notice me, and I was able to really look at his face without its usual pretense of indifference. He had long eyelashes that cast pretty shadows on his smooth cheeks. I always noticed eyelashes because that was the one feature I had that was more attractive than Mili's. Mami was always kissing my face and exclaiming over my long thick *pestañas* that, along with my dark eyes, were going to make me competitive when I became a *mujercita*. Patricio's eyelashes were too beautiful, and his curly black hair was a waste, my mother said, on a boy. It was good hair, *pelo bueno*, the kind that women on the island would kill for, shiny black and wavy. His skin was smooth as a baby's too—for now, I had heard her say, referring to the inevitable beard of the Puerto Rican man. I understood that this transformation would not be long in coming.

My female relatives were keeping their eyes on poor orphaned Patricio too, since he didn't have a mother to monitor his private life. Tía Awilda, my mother's oldest sister, had already pronounced him on the cusp of the dangerous male adolescence. She claimed to have observed a few hairs sprouting under his arms the last time she took us to the beach. "Better not let *la niña* go to Domingo's alone after dark," she had warned my mother in an ominous tone, leaving me to wonder whether Patricio grew hair all over his body after the sun set, and making me listen for howls from next door, as our bedrooms were separated by only three feet of grass and one hibiscus hedge.

It was toward these plants that we headed. Patricio had tried unsuccessfully to send me away, but I knew he was just concerned about my breaking one of Mami's rules: "You must not handle sharp objects without adult supervision." Patricio and I both knew that a hypodermic needle fell into that category. But she had not said anything about *watching* someone else handle a sharp object, and I told him so. Patricio had to admit that my argument was technically sound, but we still exercised caution in case she should show up on her quiet little feet wearing her coat of invisibility. She had taken to doing that more and more since Tía Awilda had spotted Patricio's underarm hair. She would simply walk in on us, look at us playing with our puppets, and then leave again, no explanations. She owed me none—I understood that—one of the privileges of a mother's absolute power that I would one day possess myself.

"What are you going to do?" I asked Patricio more than once as he filled the hypodermic with a light-blue solution.

But he remained silent, smiling in a way that meant I should just watch. So I followed him outside while he hid the needle in his hand. We had both seen the villain in a Charlie Chan movie do this before he injected a sleeping drug into the girl he had kidnapped.

When we got to the bush bearing the huge white hibiscus, Patricio motioned me nearer. We crouched down to examine the plant more closely.

"Here," he said, pointing to a tightly wound little bud. He traced the stem down close to the ground, then, looking just like a doctor feeling for a plump vein in a patient's arm, he chose a spot to inject the blue liquid.

"Are you killing it?" I asked in a whisper, frankly hoping that we were doing something truly forbidden, for such opportunities were rare for me. I didn't really think my cousin would be hurting one of his mother's plants, yet the needle glinted in the sunlight like the eye of a snake. In my mind, giving an injection represented pain and tears. I had just gone through the whole immunization series being pushed by an American health-and-hygiene propaganda campaign. Our school hallways were plastered with posters of smiling blond children getting stuck on their upper arms by starched, buxom, cheerful nurses—nothing like the tired health workers who stabbed us assembly-line style. The vaccination drive was making budding anarchists out of many of us healthier Puerto Rican children.

"No, I'm not killing them, niña. I'm changing them."

And though I begged, Patricio would not explain what he was doing. We made several more trips to the kitchen to refill the hypodermic with the solution. The mixture of colors changed constantly, like light refracted through a prism, a brilliant melding of possibilities.

He placed the needle on the grass near my foot. I instinctively drew back as if it could suddenly rear up and strike me like a snake. "Where did you get it?"

He shook his head, refusing to answer.

"Now we have to wait," Patricio whispered in my ear. He was close enough for me to see the little hairs sprouting over his upper lip. A shiver ran down my spine, and I wrapped my arms around his neck and put my cheek next to his skin, which smelled like my Patricio and no one else.

"Wait for what?"

"Until the flowers bloom." He nuzzled me, tickling me with his invisible mustache, rocking me like a baby in his arms.

Patricio's was the only focused attention I got that year, since Mili—so active and impulsive—was claiming most of my mother's time and energy. I had heard her tell Tía Awilda that Mili had slipped away from her at the hotel and it had taken several people combing the grounds to find her. Papi had been anguished, then embarrassed and angry with her for her *descuido*. A terrible accusation to make of any woman, that she had been careless with a child.

"It was not my fault," Mami had insisted to my aunt. "I had to let go of her hand to write down an order. *Dos segundos, nada más.*" It had taken just seconds for Mili to vanish. They had found her at the edge of the swimming pool—unaware of the chaos she had created around her, mesmerized by the play of sunlight on the water, chanting, "*Azul, azul, azul,*" while amused tourists commented on the strange little Puerto Rican girl who had never seen a swimming pool.

After that, Mami enlisted me in her vigilance of "our" Mili, who was high-strung, artistic, and needed *mucho ojo*. Our eyes were to be upon Mili until she matured and learned to control her insatiable curiosity and her propensity for putting her life in danger. Or so we hoped.

SERPIENTES and AZÚCAR

My mother and my father each had their own ideas about *la isla*, *los Estados Unidos*, *el mundo*, and *la vida*—theories they felt they ought to teach Mili and me in as dramatic a way as possible. So every Sunday, the only day Papi got off from his job at the Golden Palms Hotel, he would plan a road trip in his 1949 lime-green Studebaker. Now it is possible to go anywhere on the island in a day—it is a mere thirty-five by one hundred miles in area—but in those days, American engineers had not yet blasted through the mountains of the Cordillera Central, and all traffic—including the precariously loaded sugarcane transport trucks, rickety flatbed relics of loosely tied bundles—had to maneuver the winding ribbon of road to get to the other side. It was a narrow two-lane highway, and according to the island's macho protocol, right of way was determined by either the bigger or the faster vehicle—or the gutsiest driver.

Being a reasonable man, Papi would assess the situation according to the make, year, and condition of the approaching car or truck, as well as the set of the driver's head: hunched over the wheel meant he was suicidal and possibly homicidal. Anything less than a raging maniac Papi claimed he could handle. He'd order us to brace ourselves for a heart-stopping maneuver as he passed a slow truck that completely obscured his forward vision, or a car full of turistas, distracted by the awesome sight of a turquoise ocean to the left and a sheer drop into a bottomless abyss straight ahead. Mami would cross herself and say, "Here we go, *con Dios, María, José*, and all the saints." And my father would almost invariably respond dryly, "*Por favor, querida*, do not load this car down with so many extra passengers." This exchange elicited giggles from Mili and me in the backseat, and a dirty look from Mami, who did not approve of blasphemy even in jest.

Occasionally, Papi would be faced with an obstinate truck driver barreling down on us, and after Mami had screamed in terror a couple of times, he would swing the Studebaker off the road and partway up the mountainside, allowing his challenger to pass. He did all this calmly and quietly, unlike the other drivers whose shouting matches had Mami constantly rolling up the car windows in order to protect our innocent ears, even though that meant suffocating in the stifling heat. The *público* and *línea* drivers were particularly vicious. As the short- or long-distance taxis on the island, they got paid by how many sweaty passengers they could haul from pueblo to pueblo. These irascible men were distinguishable from others by the fact that their left arms, which hung out of the car windows all day, were usually several shades darker than the rest of their bodies. That arm was their signaling arm, and the signals they gave other cars could not always be found in a driver's manual, my mother said.

We often had blowouts and car trouble. Everyone did then. So we knew the routine when we heard the familiar pop and Papi began to maneuver the car off the paved road. Since it was sweltering hot, Mami would get out and look around to make sure it was safe, then let Mili and me escape for fresh air. She would take these occasions to point out things to us about our island as if we were turistas.

One day we had a flat by the side of a sugarcane field that extended toward the horizon like a green sea. It was ready for harvesting. *La zafra*, the cutting season, is also the time of *fiestas* on the island, and we were heading for Mami's pueblo to the festival of the town's patron saint, San Lázaro. We would stay with her mamá a few days, and Papi would return to San Juan by himself since he had to go back to work.

Mami's happiness about going to her mother's casa showed in the way she moved her body—her hips loose and her step light. In fact, the day before, she had put on a mambo record to do her mopping in anticipation of the trip. Mili and I had pranced around the house with her as she polished the floors, dancing with the mop to the sounds of Tito Puente and his orchestra.

Now, Mami's starched red cotton skirt and off-the-shoulder peasant blouse made her look like a movie star as she scanned the cane field, shading her eyes with one hand and holding both Mili's and my hands with the other. Papi's rule: If there was even the possibility of a moving vehicle in our path, we must be securely attached to an adult. At age ten, I was beginning to resent this, but Mami only obeyed Papi's excessively protective commandments when he was around. We had a silent agreement, she and I. We humored Papi in exchange for other privileges we exacted from each other. Mili had not yet caught on to these tactics; she seemed impervious to the family negotiations that went on constantly as we circled one another trying to figure out how to gain the most territory without starting a war.

"What are you looking for, Mami?" Mili asked, now six, pretty and vivacious as a Puerto Rican Shirley Temple with her mass of black curls, peach skin, and pearly white teeth. Mami could not help but hug and kiss her at least once an hour, by my rough calculations. I liked her too, but I knew she had a bad side. In fact, I had saved her from herself quite a few times. Mili was impulsive, even reckless. And I was always to blame for her mishaps, as her older sister and custodian, by default.

"I'm trying to see if the cane is ready to eat," Mami whispered, bending down to look us in the eyes. "There is nothing sweeter than *la caña* of this part of our *isla, hijas. Es pura azúcar.*" Then she crossed her lips with her finger for silence. I knew why she was speaking low. Papi did not allow us to eat anything that had not been "processed"—meaning either it bore a seal from some U.S. government inspector or he had examined the product for the worms, decay, pits, bones, or fibers that would choke his little girls; of course that meant depriving us of much of the island's bounty on which Mami had grown into the healthy woman he had married.

"Country people learn early to deal with dangers you have not faced or will not need to face," he had explained to me after forbidding me to suck on a *quenepa*, a slippery gooey fruit with a pit about the size of my gullet. One of my aunts had brought Mami a bunch from a tree in my *abuela*'s yard. Papi's "No" had been firm enough to send me crying to my room. But when he left for work, Mami had brought in a few in a paper bag, then had shown me how to curl my tongue around the *pepita* so that it would not slide down my throat, and how to suck on the flesh of the fruit and savor it while rolling the pit back and forth in my mouth. It was a complicated but satisfying way to enjoy a forbidden fruit—absolutely worth the trouble. But accepting these indulgences meant I had had to pay the price of keeping secrets—about this and about other forbidden things, such as María Sereno's manicures.

I had been so deep in thought that I jumped when I heard my sister's wild laughter and saw that she had broken loose from Mami's grasp and was running into the field. We both called her, and my father dropped the tire he was about to mount on the wheel and ran after her. He grabbed her by the arm and hurried her back to Mami.

Caught by surprise, Mili was not sure what she had done wrong. Papi looked sternly into Mami's face as he said to us, "There might be snakes in those stalks. Your mother should be a little more careful about what she promises you."

He then opened the car doors and waited for us to get settled in seats so hot that our sweat-damp dresses stuck to the vinyl covers. It took him longer than usual to change the tire. No one said anything until he eased the car back onto the *carretera militar* that circled the island in its tortuous route.

"There are no poisonous *serpientes* on our *isla*," my mother said in a tone that told us, *This is a fact, nothing more need be said about the subject.* And nothing was.

Instead, Papi pointed out the progress that had been made on the island's roads since American science and technology had arrived along with Operation Bootstrap. The plan was to transform our beautiful but primitive tropical paradise into a welcoming resort for mainland tourists, and subsequently into an attractive investment opportunity for industrialists seeking cheap labor within American borders. The first item of business was a highway through the annoyingly curvaceous central mountain range.

As we penetrated the heart of the mountains, we made what seemed like concentric circles around peaks and valleys spotted with goats and cows who seemed to defy gravity as they stood precariously munching grass on the steep hillsides. We complained of carsickness out of force of habit, since that was what Mami did every time we made the trip. Papi explained that soon, very soon, the American engineers would blast a hole right through the rock and we would be able to speed from one end of the island to the other in a fraction of the time it now took. While holding a perfume-scented handkerchief to her nose to ease her nausea, Mami made her usual passionate protest against this defacement of nature. I knew that she was echoing her papá, a nationalist and a nature lover, when she made her little speeches in which the country became personified as a beautiful woman in danger of being defiled by the rough invaders.

THE ANGEL OF DEATH

Her papá, our abuelo, had had a taste of politics during World War II, when he had become a sort of Angel to Widows and Orphans. It had been his job to break the news of a son or husband's death to the women in his pueblo, as the mayor had become grief-stricken and incapable of performing this most delicate of duties after his only son had been killed early in the war. Abuelo had stepped in at the urging of his compañeros, since he had a reputation as a mediator and peacemaker. Most of his power to persuade came from his oratorical skills and deep resonant voice cultivated during his career as a reader for the cigar makers. He would intone selections from the daily newspapers, as well as passages from the great works of literature and the Bible. The tobacconists were said to be the best-informed, most knowledgeable men in the land.

Now, in his leisure time, he declaimed. He made speeches about almost anything, but usually about the loss of autonomy of our patria, which he equated with the loss of its men's virility, and about the imminent decay of our island culture. This mission had resulted in a schism within his own family, because Abuela and her daughters were all for automation and technology. And Abuela had the deciding vote, since she was the one who had a little money—inherited from her mother, Isadora, a famous seamstress who had eventually opened her own shop, the first ready-made dress store in the pueblo.

It was Abuela who had bought the first washing machine she saw on sale. She had expressed the hope that the world was finally turning in favor of women. She had then vowed to invest in every product that allowed her the luxury she had never had as a wife and mother—time for herself. The following year she had bought a television set and the marriage had almost ended.

Abuelo raged on to the point where a noise war was declared at their casa, with Abuela turning up the volume on her TV set to the maximum, driving Abuelo to the public plaza, raging against the killers of the tongue.

"And what will you and I do without a tongue?" he shouted, as he was being swept out of his own home by the wave of mindless dialogue dubbed in Spanish pouring out of the talking box in his parlor.

"I would die of pure joy if you lost yours," Abuela would toss at him without taking her eyes off the latest episode of Perry Mason.

Whenever Abuelo was driven off, he went to the town square, where other old men gathered to tell melancholy tales of the former days of glory on the island—back when el hombre *was the lord and master of his own casa.*

When we drove up to Abuela's, we found the women sitting on the front porch. We got hugged and kissed repeatedly until Mili broke away, running to the backyard, where our boy cousins were feeding the chickens. I backed off from the adults' circle, but not too far, so

I could listen to them without being noticed. Papi stayed only long enough to drink a cup of Abuela's sweet *café con leche*. Then, smiling away Abuela's usual protests that he should not leave without eating a full meal, he drove off. He wanted to leave before Abuelo came home from his daily domino game at the plaza. If he didn't escape quickly, he'd surely be subjected to one of Abuelo's anti-American lectures. He'd be tricked into an argument one way or another. Abuelo's latest tactic was to ask my mother what new time-saving gadget Papi had bought her, and when she proudly told him of her vacuum cleaner, automatic coffee pot, or whatever, he would begin his rehearsed attack on unconscionable capitalism or the erosion of moral values due to the Americanization of our island. Mami fell for his verbal traps almost every time, since to deny her husband's gifts was a betrayal worse than putting up with her father's rantings.

As I watched the Studebaker disappear, I felt freed from Papi's constant vigilance just as Mami must have. Bored with the women's excited reunion, I sneaked off to my favorite place in the house, Abuelo's library. Settling into his old cane-back chair, I took down a history book and let it fall open to a line drawing of soldiers herding *Indios* down a road; the Indians were naked, the conquistadors in full battle dress and carrying guns. I remembered when I had first seen this book.

Because we were all together for holidays, when one of us children got sick, we all did. One Christmas we were all spotted with chicken pox and had to spend most of a week in quarantine, sharing our misery in this back suite of rooms where Abuelo kept his personal library. I had a great time looking at the well-worn books that he had read to the cigar makers. There was an illustrated *Don Quixote*, with a drawing of a skinny old man with a long nose and a pointy beard, brandishing a sword at a windmill. And there was Shakespeare in Spanish; a page starting with *Mañana, mañana y mañana* was marked with a funeral service card dated ten years before my birth.

Abuelo had visited us in our sickroom. He came in wearing his white linen suit and straw hat. He'd kissed each of our foreheads, which were smeared like the rest of us with calamine lotion, wiped his face with a clean linen handkerchief, and asked me, perhaps because he knew I loved his cuentos, if we wanted to hear him read a story. Without hesitation I answered *¡Sí!* My sister and our cousins, Miguelito, Manuelito, and Rafaelito—ten, six, and five, respectively—would have preferred, I knew, an hour of TV. But we were in quarantine, so no one was turning away any form of entertainment.

Abuelo then went over to the shelves, climbed on a step stool, and reached for a book that seemed to be falling apart from age. He pulled Abuela's rocker closer to our big bed, where we had been improvising a game of charades earlier, and showed us the cover of the yellowed book. It had an illustration of a seashore on it, just as it must have looked when the Taino Indians lived there, with stretches of white sand bordered by lush vegetation. He read us the title in his public speaking voice: *Historia y Leyendas de Puerto Rico*.

"How the Tainos discovered that their conquerors, the Spaniards, were mortal men and not Gods." Abuelo announced the title of his reading with a dramatic flourish of his right hand. The little kids squirmed around me like restless puppies. We had all been subjected to Abuelo's speeches. Mili cuddled next to me, and I could hear her beginning that soft humming that preceded either a fit of giggles or a crying jag. I put my hand lightly over her mouth to prevent any outburst. Abuelo now raised his index finger, pausing dramatically in preparation for his delivery. My boy cousins were lying motionless, their eyes fixed on a spot on the ceiling.

"In the early days of the Spanish invasion of Borinquén—as

our island was called by its original inhabitants, the peaceful Taino Indians—there was widespread belief among the natives that the Spaniards were gods. And so the Indians were easy targets for these white men with their magic spears that made fire and thunder . . ."

"Those were rifles." Miguelito could not help showing off his fifth-grade history knowledge.

Abuelo raised his finger again. He resumed his reading in a louder voice. I saw Mami and Abuela appear at the door behind his back. Mami's look said, *Stay where you are. Be quiet. Do not acknowledge me.*

"An old Indian chief who was known for his wisdom decided to see for himself if these men, whose cruelty and greed had practically destroyed the Indians' culture and broken their spirits, were really gods. He asked for several young men of his village to volunteer in an experiment that might cost them their lives." Abuelo then interrupted himself to say, "There are some ideals worth dying for, hijos."

I was watching my mother and Abuela exchange a dark look. They were going to see how far the story went before Abuelo had to be reminded that his audience was well under the voting age.

"And so this old chief waited for the opportunity to put his plan to work, and it was not long before it arose. The Spaniards were accustomed to the servitude of Indians and it did not matter whether they had seen them before—*Indios* were simply conscripted into service at the whim of the white men. And so it came to pass that a Spaniard was traveling through the old chief's territory, and he ordered the old man to provide him with some men to carry his baggage as well as himself across a river. The chief humbly agreed, as was expected of him, but in his own tongue he reminded his men of what they were to do on that day."

Abuela made her move then. She walked quietly into the room and perched herself at the foot of the bed with all of us spotted ones safely under her wing. Abuelo frowned at her and she calmly stared back at him. He cleared his throat and resumed the story.

"This was the chief's plan: the Spaniard was to be carried on the shoulders of his men to the deepest part of the river. Then they were to drop him in the water and hold him under for several hours."

Mami joined Abuela at the foot of the bed. But by now Miguelito, Manuelito, and Rafaelito were sitting up, listening. This story was getting good. Maybe a war between the Spaniards and the Indians would follow. I knew better. Abuelo's time was running out fast. He knew it too.

"Of course the plan worked." Abuelo was talking quickly now. His denouement was being ruined, but he would wrap up his story no matter what dire consequences might ensue. "The Spaniard was as dead as any drowned man ever was when the Indians dragged him to shore. The news spread fast across Borinquén's Indian villages. The invaders were not gods, they were mere mortal men!"

"*Bien*, Papá," my mother said, standing up in front of him so as to block our view, "that was a good story, but these *niños* are sick and too much excitement is not good for them. We'd better let them take a *siesta* now."

Without a word, but in his typical dignified manner, Abuelo returned the old book to its assigned place in his bookcase, and placing his straw hat firmly on his head, he walked out of our ward like a man satisfied with a job well done.

Abuela was muttering an Ave María, in an annoyed tone as if the Holy Mother had let her down again, while she rearranged us into our separate sleeping spaces with pillows.

"You will be happy to know that you will be allowed to watch television for a little while tonight, children," she announced.

We all squealed at the news and tried to hug her, but she was tucking us in tight under our cool sheets, and we knew that the payment for the gift of an hour of television was the pretense of a siesta. Mili started tickling my palms under the blanket, trying to make me laugh out loud. And as soon as the women left, I wrapped her up in a cocoon with our blanket and held her down until she stopped giggling and fell asleep.

But the chicken pox scars had faded, and my memories of that past Christmas were shelved along with the book I carefully returned to its allotted spot in Abuelo's library. It was August now, and Mami had promised to take us to the fiestas during this visit to Abuela's. The thick green forests and the lonely paths where the *leyendas* of our island were enacted by men and women long dead had nothing to do with the bright lights, music, and carnival rides I was looking forward to that night.

At dusk the sensory world of the small pueblo fell like a mosquito net over us. We were instantly wrapped in our roles as *mujercitas*, little women, and *hombrecitos*, little men. The women dressed us for our parts so that we could parade to the fiestas in the plaza like the *gente decente* we were. That meant that we had to wear our most uncomfortable good clothes, even though it was a dusty walk down to the paved road and we would be getting on carnival rides that were sure to leave permanent stains on the starched pink-and-yellow dresses that flounced over our skinny legs like crinoline mushrooms.

"*Adiós, adiós,*" we called, waving to our neighbors as we passed by their houses. We said it in that special tone that meant neither hello nor good-bye, but rather that let them know we were on our way to a special place: Look at us, don't we look fine? And the women smiled in approval and nodded their heads at our abuela, which meant "*Sí, señora,* that is how children should look. How fortunate you are to have such a good-looking *familia.*"

We knew our roles by now. On our best behavior, we were to follow Abuela and her daughters like ducklings in a row to the plaza, where we would be reviewed by the public—neighbors and relatives who had not seen us regularly and who had to be allowed to exclaim over our body parts: "*¡Qué guapos!* Rafaelito has such a fine head of hair. Manuelito is going to be a lady-killer with those ebony eyes. Miguelito, he is practically *un hombre grande ya.*" After the *machitos* had been praised, Mili and I would come under scrutiny. Mili got the compliments on her anatomy, but I would be praised for my seriousness. I always had Mili by the hand when my mother didn't, since we never knew when she'd take off running once something caught her eye. So Mami always said that I was her *mano derecha* when it came to Mili, her right hand. And, as if I were not standing there, sometimes neighbors would ask Mami if I was already developing. I knew they meant breasts and hair under my arms like the hair my cousin Patricio was growing. It sent shivers down my spine to think that this would happen to me. It was only after we paid the penance of this public ritual that we were allowed to roam around the plaza, where there were dozens of eyes to watch us, and any adult present was automatically responsible for taking care of any child in his or her view. There were few dangers, or so it seemed.

The plaza was a fantasyland during the fiestas, set off from the reality of the rest of the pueblo by a ring of multicolored lights. It contained the new carnival rides we dreamed of all year long. Each year we were allowed to progress from the easy rides to the more dangerous ones—from the carousel, to the bumper cars, to the Ferris wheel. Someday we would enter the show inside the tent, or at least the boys would, since Abuela said the spectacle was nothing but vulgar slapstick comedy and half-naked women showing their panties. I saw Manuelito's eyes get big whenever Abuela berated the tent show, but it was in fascination, not horror.

There were kiosks that sold *bacalaítos*, the salty codfish fritters Mami liked so much but didn't make often because Papi said they filled the house with a smell he hated, one of salty, greasy fried fish. Mami claimed that *bacalao* was island food, implying that to reject it was to reject his heritage. No one ever won the argument over *bacalao*.

For the children there were hard coconut *turrones* and soft candies made of guava, mango, and the tart orange that I had tasted from Abuela's tree. That tree grew over the bedroom I slept in. During the night its fruit dropped like rocks on the zinc roof. I had for a time believed that this sound was caused by the bully who lived in the two-story house across from Abuela's, who liked to throw stones at our house. He was fifteen and known to be an odd bird. No one could control Néstor, who already drank rum and was rumored to have hit his own mother. We were all waiting for the day when he would be taken off to jail. In the meantime we were supposed to act like we knew nothing about Néstor's vices because Abuela was his *madrina*, godmother, which made his mother and our abuela practically relatives, with a bond between them that the priest had blessed in church, a bond that was, therefore, as irrevocable as marriage.

And because it seemed safe to let go of Mili's hand within the magic circle of adults watching us from the perimeters of the plaza, I left her with the boys while I rode the Ferris wheel, a new privilege that year. I got seated next to a girl I didn't know, a fact I enjoyed since I wanted to concentrate on the experience without having to share it. I held my breath as I rose above the people below, until I saw only the tops of their heads moving like pieces in a Chinese checkers game—black heads, white heads. At the top the ride was stopped while others got on, and I looked around for my family. I spotted the women in a small group drinking something, probably *maví*, from paper cones that looked like pointy party hats held upside down. Then I turned toward the spot where I had left Mili and my cousins with tickets for the carousel. I saw the three boys right away. They were in line for the bumper cars, but Mili was not with them.

My heart started pounding as I twisted and turned, looking everywhere for my sister. The girl next to me held on to the sides, obviously upset at my abrupt movements. She gave me a dirty look. I ignored her, turning all the way around in my seat. The ride resumed with a jerk and on the way down past the dark area behind the rides I finally saw Mili.

She was behind a kiosk sitting on Néstor's lap, eating an ice-cream cone. He was holding a cigarette in one hand and holding her like a large doll with his other hand hidden behind her back. When I saw—or did I just think I saw?—what he was doing to my sister, I yelled out her name as loud as I could. The girl next to me said harshly, "*¿Estás loca?* What are you doing? Do you want to get us killed?" But I kept on yelling Mili's name until finally she looked up. I didn't believe that she could really hear me above all the noise, but I saw her leap from Néstor's lap and run toward the Ferris wheel. When I passed her on my way up again, I shouted, "Mili, wait for me right there. Wait for me!" She waved back with her ice-cream cone, spilling the chocolate all over the front of her white dress. From where I was, it looked like a blood stain, and my head throbbed as I felt myself getting sick to my stomach.

"I knew I shouldn't have agreed to let you get on the Ferris wheel. If your father had been here we would all be in trouble now." My mother wiped my face with her perfumed handkerchief.

"She's older than Rafaelito and he went on," Tía Awilda said, in an almost boastful tone.

"But he's an *hombrecito*," Abuela pointed out, smoothing back my hair. "Girls are more delicate."

"I'm fine!" I pushed my mother's hands away. I was embarrassed to be babied in public. Their effusive concern was even worse than the stares I got when I threw up as I got off the Ferris wheel. At least I had managed to hold it until then. No one praised me for that. Mili ran to get Mami and by the time they all got there Néstor had vanished—and so had my courage. I could not tell my mother about what I had allowed to happen. The *pueblo chiquito* system of adult supervision had failed. I had failed. I convinced myself that Néstor had just bought Mili a cone, and that he was Abuela's neighbor, practically family. Mili seemed to have forgotten the incident; at least she didn't say anything about it. Abuela declared that the niñas should go home with her and Mami since we were not presentable and I obviously needed one of her *guarapos* to settle my stomach. *Los niños* could stay with their mothers and enjoy the fiesta. Another rule for a *mujer decente*: If one gets in trouble, we all pay.

When we arrived home, Abuelo was sitting in a rocker on the porch reading. He laid the book on his lap in order to kiss us. I saw that it was by Homer, the story of a sailor-king and his adventures. I asked him to read to me.

"I don't think she needs more excitement, Papá," my mother said.

But because being sick gives one certain privileges, I cuddled up to the old man who had the voice of a prophet, letting him comfort me like a baby.

"I will read to her from a classical work, hija. No upsetting politics for my Consuelito. Do not worry." He took my hand and led me to the room with the bookshelves. As big as I was, I crawled into his lap and put my head inside his suit where it was dark and aromatic of his special cologne and cigars and coffee. I listened to Abuelo gather the power of his voice deep inside his chest.

"Once upon a long ago time, on an island, like our island, there lived a powerful king named Odysseus. He was wise, courageous, and kind. He lived in a great castle with his faithful wife, Penelope. Their lives were peaceful until the woman, Helen, caused the war of Troy by her betrayal of her husband and homeland, and this is the story." Abuelo was extemporizing for me; I knew it because I had taken that book down one day and read many pages. Ever since the time of the chicken pox, I often sneaked into this room while the others were taking a siesta. I looked through Abuelo's books one after the other, memorizing each one's place on the bookshelf by the color of the leather cover or the size of the book, since weeks might pass before I came back to my grandparents' house. I was looking for one that would tell the story of girls or queens who had lives as interesting as those of Odysseus, Don Quixote de la Mancha, or even real people like the Puerto Rican heroes mentioned in a book with drawings of bearded men in high collars.

"Odysseus left the faithful Penelope at home on the island when he went to fight in the Trojan War." I gave myself over to the story of the great warrior king Odysseus, whom I imagined as an older version of Patricio, and his loyal wife who waited at home, Penelope. *Una mujer decente*, if there ever was one. I wanted to hear more about Odysseus's travels. But my mind wandered away from this perfect man and his constant wife. It was instead Abuelo's familiar voice, a sound like distant thunder heard from the safety of one's own bed, that put me in a trance like a kitten carried in its mother's mouth, both caught and safe. I pressed my ear to his chest so I could feel the deep vibrations of his voice and I placed my palm on his throat as he enunciated each word and I dreamed myself into his tales. I was the hero, the one wearing the heavy armor of the good knight, and I rescued my sister from many disasters in my dreams, even though it was bone-wrenching torture to climb those towers where she was held by the enemy.

I buried my face in Abuelo's fresh-smelling starched *guayabera*, wishing away my floating fears about everything, and I slept. I dreamed—but not about Odysseus who outsmarted even the gods, nor even about his forbearing wife, Penelope. I dreamed about unnamed threats—about what Odysseus told the vanquished Cyclops to call him: Nobody. I remember it as my grandfather said it in his resonant Spanish, *"Nadie, soy Nadie."* I am Nobody, Nobody! And so, the Cyclops, his one eye blinded by the man who called himself Nobody, cursed and yelled at the wind and the sea ruled by his brother, Poseidon. And when Poseidon asked him who did this, he responded: *"Nadie, Nadie.* Nobody blinded me. Nobody."

¡AY BENDITO!: Betrayals of the Tongue

The trip home began in tense silence. There were things not to be spoken of, mainly about Mili. I had heard her get up in the night and had heard Mami's soft voice cajoling her out of somewhere—from under a table, out of a closet. Mili liked to hide in small spaces when she was afraid. I would have normally followed Mami's voice, led Mili back into bed with me. But I had stayed under my covers last night, hoping I wouldn't be pulled from my refuge.

As the silence in the stifling hot car grew heavier, Papi began a guided tour using the deep voice of a radio announcer: here are the factories, the shopping centers, and housing developments springing up, in, and around the bigger pueblos on the island. He wanted to show us the model home that had just opened to the public; he hoped to buy one someday using his GI loan. It was just beginning to get dark when we pulled into a paved driveway with a square cement house partially painted pink. The paint looked weathered, as if someone had run out of it and abandoned the project. In front there was a sign announcing the area as the future site of El Camino Terrace. My mother asked what *Terrace* meant, and when Papi told her, she shook her head.

"The name does not make sense. Where is there a veranda, or a patio? That is what a terrace is, no? This is a cement box sitting on a flat lot. The name, this Terrace, it's a joke by *los americanos*, right?"

"It's just a name, Angélica," my father said, herding us all toward the cement-block and tile porch.

It irritated him that Mami often felt compelled to comment on the absurd combinations of Spanish and English words now popping up everywhere on the island's billboards and signs. It was as if it did not matter to the developers that the names of their housing projects, combining English and Spanish, sometimes resulted in nonsense.

Papi picked Mili up and deposited her on the porch since there were no steps yet and her legs did not quite reach. As soon as he set her down she let out a piercing scream.

"*¿Qué pasa?*" Mami and I ran up the drive. We thought a bee had stung her or something had bitten her. Mili had wrapped her legs around Papi and was staring down in terror.

But Papi was laughing quietly. He pointed to the porch floor, covered from end to end with a multitude of frogs. They were all crowded together like a congregation of fat old ladies at Sunday mass—a chorus, Papi explained, that had fallen silent when we drove up.

"That's because we are intruding in their territory," my mother said, not smiling.

"Angélica, if you don't watch out you will become a boring *Independentista*, like your father. You're beginning to sound just like him." My father's smile had disappeared. He took Mili's hand and led us through the cool cement house, which was perfectly square, the rooms fitted like little boxes inside a big box. The kitchen was equipped with modern appliances that Mami examined carefully. When she opened the oven door a frog hopped out. Mami fell into Papi's arms laughing. "*Dios mío*, I almost had a heart attack," she exclaimed. "These *ranas* are a nuisance." We all laughed while Mili and I chased the frog out to the porch, where he joined his friends and relatives in silence.

Back on the road my parents discussed money in hushed voices. I peered out the window as night fell. The lights of the power plants looked like futuristic space stations to me. I had grown up seeing only the distant twinkling of house lights in the pueblos, lights that receded like the stars as we climbed higher into the mountains. Everything was changing so fast. Now there were new smells in the air too, from the petroleum refineries. They overwhelmed the familiar thick aroma of sugarcane that had once permeated the breezes. New electrically generated sounds from the plants and factories drowned out the music of the *coquís* except in pueblos deep in the countryside. The *coquís* don't like to compete. They fall silent when a TV is turned on, or a car engine is revved up, or any other sound interrupts their hymn to the night. Abuelo had warned that the day the *coquís* stopped singing forever, Puerto Rico would no longer be Puerto Rico.

The morning after we got back from Abuela's, I ran over to Patricio's house. I knocked on the kitchen door, but no one answered. I went around to his window, but the Venetian blinds were rolled shut. I ran my fingers over the blinds in our secret code, once up, once down. I heard him moving around.

"Consuelo?"

"Let me in, Patricio."

I had been so concerned with being locked out that I had not stopped to look at the hibiscus bush behind me. When I turned around I caught my breath in surprise. The flowers had blossomed! The white hibiscus of his mother's garden were now mixed with strange and wonderful offspring in deep variations of blue: purple with gold undertones, electric blue, lavender with red veins, and delicate powder blue. I was transfixed, stunned by the revelation that it was possible to change nature.

"Come in, Consuelo." Patricio's voice through the blinds sounded a little strange, hoarse, choked, as if he had been crying. I ran to him and kissed his face. It always made me feel full of joy to see him—even after the briefest separation. But something seemed wrong this time. His hug was halfhearted and his eyes distant.

After I had blurted out my amazement at, and admiration for, his "Martian garden," as I decided to call it, Patricio told me what had happened two days ago, when the first flowers had opened.

"It was Mario Manuel who started the trouble." Patricio looked a little like his father when he said this—I mean, he turned his eyes away as he spoke. I sat Indian-style in front of him and took his hands in mine like we did when we had our serious talks.

"You mean María Sereno?"

"That's not his real name, Consuelo."

"That's what everybody calls him," I insisted, thinking that Patricio didn't know the whole story about how Mario had turned into María.

"Not everybody." He sounded annoyed, a very unusual tone for my sweet cousin. So I said softly, "Tell me what happened."

Apparently it had been María Sereno who had spotted the first purple-and-gold hibiscus. He had squealed in such delight that the women whose nails he had been working on hurried over to look at Patricio's creation. Patricio had been in his room at the time and had heard the comments they had made about him.

"Like what?"

"You would not understand, Consuelito. You are too young."

To my shock I saw tears rolling down Patricio's face. I wiped them off with one of the pretty pieces of gold cloth strewn on the floor around us. "If those women don't think your flowers are out of this world, they are stupid."

"Hey! You're messing up Mrs. Smit's ball gown." He took the gold lamé from my hand and wiped his face with his shirtsleeve. He showed me how he had started to make a costume for our irritating turista doll, Mrs. Smith from New York City. Her name was mispronounced by the Puerto Rican puppets as *la Misis Smit*. He smiled at me, but I knew that whatever the neighbors had said had hurt him deeply.

"Mario Manuel stole one of my flowers. He put it behind his ear to show off."

"I don't like him."

"He's not a bad person, Consuelo." Patricio's surprising defense of María Sereno confused me. Patricio was right. I still didn't understand how older people could see one another as enemies one minute and friends the next: like my parents, who seemed to disagree about almost everything, yet Mami turned into a lioness when anyone said anything bad about her Carlos.

"He stole your flower."

"I think he thought he was standing up for me by admiring it in front of the others."

I gave up trying to see the logic in the situation. I decided to allow all this to sink in later when I was in my room alone, reading my grown-up books and thinking about what happened. I didn't always come up with answers, but sometimes, if I carefully went over words I had heard, a little flash would go off in my head. For now, I was caught up in the aura of romance and adventure that was all around Patricio when he created new stories for us. I wanted to see how the cotton-haired, bespectacled Mrs. Smit would look in her gold lamé evening dress. María Magdalena, the maid, always outdid her, but Mrs. Smit never knew it.

My mother looked at me strangely when I came home from Patricio's. Papi had been sitting at the kitchen table across from her; I could tell because his empty coffee cup was there along with an ashtray with one lipstick-stained, filtered cigarette—hers—and one crushed Chesterfield—his. Something important must be up, I thought, for them to be in conference so early in the morning.

"Sit down, Consuelo." Mami pointed to my father's empty chair with a no-nonsense look on her face. I tried to prepare myself for what might be coming. I was certain it had to do with my neglect of Mili at the fiesta, and I trembled at the thought, remembering the evil Néstor. Many times I had heard my mother say to one of her women friends that if a man dared to touch one of her girls, Papi would kill him.

"Consuelo, your Papi and I have been discussing your *primo*."

"Which cousin? Miguelito, Manuelito, or Rafaelito?" I knew she meant Patricio, but I was trying to gain some time for myself. What had Patricio done wrong? He hardly ever left the house after school; he made straight A's in all his subjects. It had to be the flowers! He had upset them by changing his mother's flowers.

"I'm referring to Patricio Signe. Be quiet and listen to my question. Think before you answer, niña." My mother had lit another Salem and was leaning forward into the mentholated smoke. Her squinting eyes looked menacing through the cloud that divided us.

"Does anyone else besides you go into the house?"

"*El tío,*" I answered, knowing full well that was not what she meant.

"Consuelo, you are being ignorant on purpose, *malcriada*. If you won't act your age and answer my questions properly, I'll let your father do this."

"Why are you asking me these questions about Patricio, Mami? Is he in trouble?"

"I am asking the questions, niña, and I don't have to explain why to you." She slammed down the heavy gold lighter Papi had brought her from Japan.

"No. I haven't seen anyone."

"You have seen no one else there with him, ever?"

"Like who?"

"Like anyone, Consuelo. Anyone not in the family."

"Doña Graciela." I was proud of myself for being able to come up with a name, though I had a feeling that it still wasn't the answer she wanted from me.

"She's the housekeeper, not a stranger. Anyone else?"

I could tell that my mother was uncomfortable about this interrogation. I suspected Papi had given her the ultimatum: either you talk to her or I will.

"Any strange . . . men?" She exhaled a cloud of cigarette smoke as she spoke. I was glad I couldn't see her face behind the smoke, and she couldn't see mine.

"No," I said, swallowing hard and choking a little on the smoke. "I haven't seen any *strange* men there." My tone was petulant, and she nodded her head at me, a subtle warning that I was dangerously trying her patience.

"*Está bien*, Consuelo. Breakfast is almost ready. Go wash your hands and get Mili."

Had I lied? No, I told myself. I had simply chosen not to tell about the person I thought I saw slipping into Patricio's house by the back door. Perhaps I had imagined it, been fooled by a shadow as I crossed over the bushes into my own backyard. And perhaps I had not heard the slap-slap of flip-flops other than mine. It could have been only one silhouetted figure at Patricio's window, not a couple like I thought I saw when I turned toward my cousin's room at the sound of squeaking of blinds rolling shut.

Soon after my mother's interrogation of me, I heard that Tío had made Patricio dig up the hibiscus bush with its strange and beautiful blossoms, and had hacked it to pieces with a machete. I saw it piled on the sidewalk in front of his house so that the new truck that collected trash would chew it up and swallow it the next day. I ran to get a purple blossom that had survived almost intact. I dried it between the pages of the white First Communion Bible Abuela had given me. In time it became my magical page marker, endowed with powers of revelation. I would sometimes change its location with my eyes closed, allowing the book to fall open where it would, as a sort of game or ritual, to see where it would go and what words it would point to. The first time I did this, it came to rest on the story of King David spying on Bathsheba as she washed herself. I read it with a strange new feeling of excitement. It was the day before my eleventh birthday, and when we went to take a bath that night, I noticed that my chest was not completely flat anymore. I traced the subtle swelling with my fingers. Breasts sprouting like the tight little buds on the bush Patricio had injected and transformed. I inspected myself in the mirror while standing on my toes so I could see my whole body. I decided I'd let my hair grow long, past my shoulders, maybe down to my waist. Until then Mami had it cut in a pageboy because it was easier to take care of. Papi liked it short. Unlike most Puerto Rican men, he appreciated a modern look in women. But suddenly I felt I needed an extra layer of protection, a curtain that I could use to hide my face and body if I needed to. I did not like the thought that I could be so easily spied on and revealed in my nakedness.

My time with Patricio was strictly curtailed after the hibiscus incident. I could tell we were being monitored. Papi mentioned that his brother was considering a move to Nueva York. Patricio seemed removed from it all and increasingly reluctant to play with me. I asked where the puppets and science kit were, but he just shrugged his shoulders. His room had been cleared of toys and in their place there was a large bookcase with a set of the *Encyclopaedia Britannica* in English. He was teaching himself the language and practicing it by watching TV shows in English. He would put a strip of masking tape over the screen where the subtitles usually appeared so he wouldn't be tempted to read them. I asked him if he would teach me while he was learning, so that English lessons could become my excuse for seeing him more often. I was already feeling anxiety about this possible separation which Patricio suddenly seemed so eager for. It was my first hint about the true nature of love: it is not always returned in full measure. How could he want to leave our island and me?

For his fifteenth birthday, Patricio's father had given him a set of long-playing record albums and workbooks that covered the basics of conversational English. He agreed to tutor me one hour a day, outside, in his backyard, where Mami could watch us from her kitchen. While we practiced our lessons, Patricio showed me the glass-domed lizard house he had built. It was hidden from view by a large banana tree at the back of the property. After first making sure that my mother was busy hanging clothes and unable to see us from behind the bed sheets, Patricio removed the dry banana leaves from on top of the glass palace. Inside were two tiny lime-green chameleons that could change to gold, brown, blue, and almost red, according to where you put them. If you could catch them. They were swift and could slither up a wall as if they had suction cups on their feet. Patricio told me that these two had come into his room through the blinds. He'd found them clinging to the window ledge as if frozen by indecision. So he'd had this idea to make them a place out of some glass he had found in a closet. The cathedral dome was fashioned from square panes glued together in a geometric design. One of the panels was removable so that Patricio could feed his pets.

"What do they eat?" I asked as I peered through the glass.

"Insects." Patricio produced a matchbox from his shirt pocket. In it were several dead *moscas*. He shook the flies out and they landed like manna from heaven. But the lizards didn't bother to jump at the chance of a free meal. In fact they still seemed to be frozen in their tracks, their lidless, staring eyes fixed on the two giant faces looking down at them from the glass dome over their world.

"Don't they need water?"

"Look." Patricio pointed to the other side of the sphere. Through a pane he had painted a translucent blue, I saw that he had made them a tiny pond lined with a glass mosaic floor. It was made from an old souvenir ashtray of his mother's, Patricio explained, and he had "planted" a plastic palm tree that had PUERTO RICO ENCHANTS ME on it in gold letters. Smooth white stones were arranged like chaise lounges all around the blue lizard pool.

"It's beautiful." I was enthralled by this fantasy, even if the two lucky lizards were not.

"It's the Golden Palms Lizard Hotel and Lounge," Patricio said in English, hurriedly covering his creation with the dry leaves—a perfect camouflage since it looked like the foliage had fallen out of the tree and settled in a mound. Mami had finished hanging her clothes and was removing the carpenter's apron she wore to carry clothespins. Patricio and I moved swiftly to the other side of the banana tree and sat down with our English manual. Mami waved at me and shouted "Hello!" in English.

"Hello, Mother!" I waved back. She went in the house to sit at the table with her radio turned up loud to her favorite news show, *Noticiero Nacional*. I said to Patricio in a whisper, "Shouldn't we sit somewhere else? She might come over."

"Consuelito, always remember this: the best place to hide something from others is in front of their noses. Most people never see the obvious."

"Why, explain to me please, Patricio?" I asked in English, a language that was coming very easily to me. But he didn't have a chance to answer. His father had driven up and my cousin had jumped to his feet like someone caught committing a crime. Without a word to us, Tío went into the house, slamming the screen door behind him. Patricio followed, head bowed, wiping imaginary dirt off his pants and tucking his curls behind his ears like someone about to face a surprise inspection. I wanted to protect him from whatever he feared in that house, but I had no power.

And so, over and over again I said, "I love you, Patricio," as if the new English words were an incantation or a prayer.

ESCÁNDALOS and Other Commotions

That year after the lizards and the blue hibiscus was also the year they began work on the *autopista*, the modern highway that blasted through the mountains from one end of the island to the other, and my uncle finally decided it was a seller's market. He began to make plans to sell his house and move to New York. That meant that before long we would be renting our house from a stranger and I would lose my best friend and confidant. Tío told everyone that it was because real estate prices had never been higher—everyone wanted to move to or near San Juan now that they were predicting that you could cut across the island in two or three hours. But in my house we knew that Patricio's strange behavior over the last year and the gossip it was engendering were the real reasons for my uncle's decision.

At some point, without any warning, Patricio simply stopped attending school. His father didn't check on him; apparently, it was just easier for everyone to ignore the matter. Only I knew—at least I thought I was alone in knowing—that he was suffering the taunts of his schoolmates and the hostile indifference of his teachers. He said that this was because he refused to join the snobbish social cliques of boys interested only in drinking beer and rum and in pursuing giggly girls. This seemed unfair to me and I determined to learn all I could about Patricio's situation so that somehow I could help him. I listened even more closely to my parents when they were discussing Patricio's problems with my mother's sister and her husband. It was then that I began to see language as a weapon of destruction, as well as of self-defense.

My mother had asked me to make coffee for our company. Having started menstruating, I had new duties now. I was a *señorita*. All the women in my mother's family became señoritas at an early age, I was told with pride by my aunt, as if it were a rare treat to start bleeding without cause every few weeks. Finally the purpose of the menstrual bleeding was explained to me: *So I could have children and carry out God's will; so I could fulfill myself as a woman!* Then I was warned as to the many things I could not and should not do—an endless list of warnings. After that my mother, her sisters, and I piled into the car for the closing ceremony of going to the drugstore to buy sanitary pads, recognizable from fifty yards away in their bright blue box with a big white rose on the front. On the way home a final warning: the monthly bleeding and pain are things a woman never talks about in front of *los hombres*, not even *tu papá*. I did not ask any questions. I wanted them to drop the subject. But Mami insisted on telling my *cuento*, what had become my coming-of-age story.

"She thought she was hurt from a fall she took running after Mili, can you imagine?" Mami laughed, shaking her head at me since I was now expected to join the women at coffee and gossip, even about myself apparently.

"*Pero*, Angélica, you should have warned her it was coming.

You know all of us got our periods early. I was just ten, years younger than our Consuelo." Tía Divina held the record for early menses in the family and she never let any of the women forget it. I was twelve.

"Now we have a señorita in the house," my mother said proudly. Then they discussed how Mili was already a voluptuous little thing with curves where I had angles and soft flesh where I had sharp bones. They divided the compliments between us: pretty/mature; cute/smart; spontaneous and creative / thoughtful and dependable. I got all the unglamorous attributes, but was given an equal number, which was apparently what counted in being a fair parent: an equal amount of everything, good and bad; the quality of the praise was not a relevant issue.

The women had joined the men in our living room, which shone like a lake of pink glass since Mami had polished the Cuban tiles with *mucho gusto* as she danced to her Mirta Silva recordings just that morning.

I retreated toward the porch, where Mili was constructing a house from wooden tongue depressors and glue, talking to herself in a language she was inventing, adding new sounds every day. Mami thought it showed how creative she was, and told us that when she was a young girl, she and her friends talked in a secret tongue, pig Spanish. They added the prefix *chi* to each syllable and said the words so fast that their parents couldn't understand them. It was especially useful when they wanted to talk about boys. She gave us an example: "*Chi-yo chi-ten-chi-go chi-un chi-no-chi-vio.* I have a boyfriend." I had no problem deciphering the childish code, but I didn't tell her, since she seemed so proud of her youthful deviousness.

But Mili's personal vocabulary bore no relation to any language I knew about. It was tonal like Chinese and involved clicks of the tongue like nothing I had heard before. Yet she was consistent; I had heard her make the same sounds as she repeated her actions. It *was* weirdly original, maybe even brilliant, and I tried to see it like Mami did, but for some reason I didn't quite understand, I found my sister's gibberish alarming.

As I watched Mili babble to herself, I listened to the adults in the living room. "Don Domingo should have stayed home with the boy more after María Dolores died. It's a real *tragedia.*" My aunt shook her head sadly after speaking the word *tragedia*—a most serious word reserved for qualifying devastating circumstances.

"It's more of an *escándalo* than a *tragedia. Tener un hijo pato* . . ." my father said. He emphasized the slang for homosexual, *pato*: it means "a duck," and it is a cruel reference to the way effeminate boys walk, supposedly waddling like ducks. His voice was angry and his tone sarcastic. I glanced at him to see if he was chewing on his mustache yet. He was. Gnawing on his thick black mustache was what he did when he was fuming about something.

"Did somebody actually see him at *los baños* with their own eyes?" My mother glanced at me when she said this. I knew that she knew that I was listening, but she had not yet reached the decision to send me out of hearing range on some made-up errand. These days she had to balance her demands on me with the protocol involved in my now being a señorita. Almost a woman, I could hear certain things; still at twelve I *shouldn't* hear others. So instead of simply being ordered away, I got sent for a cup of coffee, a pack of cigarettes left in another room, whatever she could think of to get rid of me with my "radar ears" as she called my apparent ability to hear private conversations across rooms and through cement walls. This time I had let her know that I knew what she was doing by starting for the kitchen before she even said a word.

"Now she can read my thoughts too!"

"Then you don't need to send me away since I know what you're going to say before you say it."

"Go make a pot of coffee, Consuelo."

I kept my radar ears tuned in for the phrase *los baños*. The natural hot springs of Coamo, a site that had been used continuously for its curative powers since the native Taino Indians. Then, during the colonization, the Spaniards had built a bathing area, a place where, in the hot mineral waters springing constantly from deep in the earth, the *caballeros* could restore themselves after a long day of gold digging or rampaging through Borinquén. Now there was a hotel where the American tourists came to enjoy the curative powers of *los baños* for a price. The old pool made of ancient bricks and stones was still open to the public. But most people went to the modern section, since the Spanish *baños* were located in an isolated wooded area often littered with empty liquor bottles and worse.

"Either him or his identical twin," my father said. "I heard it from Chachi, the boy who cleans the pool at the hotel. He saw the boy and *el fulano* together."

El fulano or *la fulana*. What they call people too low on their morality scale to even mention by name. But this time I knew who *el fulano* was.

"Chachi is not the most reliable source," my mother said quietly, measuring how far she could go in contradicting my father before he stormed out of the room.

"Chachi is one of them too. *¡Un mariquita también. Malditos sean!*" Tío Yayo blurted out. Damn fags. It made his wife's jaw drop in shock. A Pentecostal who rarely said anything not preceded or followed with a Bible quotation, my uncle had surprised everyone with his un-Christian outburst, but red-faced, he got back in character quickly. "*El Señor* has spoken clearly on this matter. The Bible states . . ."

"We know El Señor's opinion about this, Agustín," my aunt interrupted on cue, using my uncle's formal name. She was not an *Aleluya*, as all of us not "in the faith" called the Pentecostals because their rowdy church services were noisy with singing and ecstatic shouts of *Aleluya, Aleluya!*

The Aleluyas all acted as if they were best friends with *El Señor Dios*, and had a private telephone line to God's big casa in the sky. Tía Divina put up with it because *la religión* had changed her husband from an abusive alcoholic into a boring, but basically nonviolent, zealot, and when it suited her, she quoted their dictums. Fortunately for the family, Tío Yayo was not a communicative man, and he usually fell asleep reading the Bible, so he was limited in his arguments to a few well-worn quotations of a general nature, which he applied to every situation. Tía Divina took up the slack, however.

"I hope Domingo can get that poor boy straightened out in Nueva York," my aunt said in a mournful tone. Clearly, in her mind, we should all pity an orphan, a boy without a mother, who had had little chance of growing up right. The few moral virtues men had, they learned from their mothers or their wives. That was a given.

"The Church . . ." My uncle started to make his usual suggestion for righting all the ills of society; but my mother was already rising from her rocker. It was four o'clock and time to make *café* again.

"*Bueno*, it may be the only thing to do, to get him away from the bad influences." She looked pointedly at my father when she said this, and he stopped chewing on his mustache to stare back at her as if to say, *Don't push me, woman,* which is what he would have said aloud if we didn't have company.

Alone in the yard Mili sang. It was like an aria in an opera about love and *tragedia*. The sounds she made were wails of pure emotion. But they were not cries for help. She was celebrating or mourning something we were not a part of. Maybe she was composing an opera called *Milagros* in her private tongue. As her voice rose and fell, everyone remained silent in the living room. Could they see *la tragedia* in the making? Why didn't anyone speak the word this time? They had so much to say about Patricio, and about every little event in the family's life. Why not now? *This is a tragedia,* someone could have said, *a tragedia happening right in front of our noses.* Mami would have cried and asked for help. Her sisters would have comforted her. Someone might have come up with a plan. But perhaps this was too painful to put into words. Perhaps it's impossible to say to a mother, Your child is sick beyond our help. She needs help we cannot give her. The *familia* cannot save her.

And so nothing was said. Eventually Mami came to stand behind me at the kitchen window. Her hand on my head shook as we both watched Mili do her ritualistic pantomime, like a medium channeling spirits, then just as suddenly becoming a little girl playing with sticks.

"Mili, time to come in and wash your hands."

"Mili, come eat some cookies, *mi amor.*"

"*Hija, ven,* come here to me, *por Dios.*"

Mami could not bring Mili in with her voice. So I went to get my sister. But when I kneeled to raise her up, Mili laughed and ran toward the kitchen door where Mami stood waiting to catch her. Her giggling was contagious and soon we were both laughing at nothing. Mami looked at us and shook her head as if to dispel her fears. She had tears in her eyes, but she smiled as she watched us tumble into the kitchen where we wrestled on the cool tile floor trying to tickle each other. "Be good, be good girls." It was obviously a relief to her to hear us laughing together again.

A dog dug up the lizard hotel. I was the one who discovered the devastation since I took it upon myself to check on Lucy and Desi, the chameleon couple who had not changed colors since moving into their crystal palace. We had carpeted their quarters with green leaves and painted the pebbles in primary colors, but they had remained a greenish gray. They didn't even move much, just sat there looking up at us looming over them, watching us in total indifference as we changed their little world. I was afraid they'd starve since I never saw them eat, but I counted the dead insects we dropped in, and some did disappear. Yet in spite of their luxurious surroundings and free meals, Lucy and Desi were always listless.

I actually cried out "No!" when I saw the pieces of glass scattered everywhere, the blue pool full of mud, all our efforts at beauty ruined. Although I looked for blood, dismembered tails and limbs, or any other signs of a violent death for Lucy and Desi, I didn't find anything to suggest that the dog had finished his dirty deed. I searched all around Tío's backyard, where the vegetation was taking over now that Tía was not around to tend it. Even in the modern suburbs of San Juan the wild tropical fruit trees and flowers had to be held back with a firm hand or they would take over. Abuelo always said the same thing when he read about new construction on the island: that the Taino Indians hardly had to lift a finger to eat well in Borinquén before the *conquistadores* arrived, for the island was like a nurturing mother whose *olla* of legumes and viands was bottomless and bountiful. If you let the land feed you, it would, and so would the sea; but nothing could grow through cement and steel. Papi usually commented to us that people who believed such romantic nonsense should quit their jobs and go live in the hills.

I looked around the frangipani tree, all through its bunched yellow flowers, and I excavated the composting mounds of dead banana tree leaves we had used as camouflage—but found nothing. Lucy and Desi were not there, they were not clinging to the leafy trunk of the banana tree that had stood guard over their glass castle, nor were they scampering around the hedge of hibiscus bushes that separated Tío's yard from ours. But I knew that they were not dead; I had a strong sense that they were just hiding from me, having transformed themselves into part of a twig or a leaf, something obvious, right under my nose, where I could not see them. There was that feeling when I entered my house these days too; there was something living among us that we were not yet able to fully acknowledge, a kind of fearful expectation.

The Meaning of the Word TRAGEDIA

For the next two years our household was relatively peaceful. My parents seemed to have reached an understanding in their relationship; most of their discussions now seemed to center on whether Tío Domingo would finally make the move to Nueva York as he had been promising for so long. My father continued to convert Mami to the American way of life by introducing us to the latest technical and electronic wonders from the mainland.

One day Mili and I came home from school to catch my father in the act of throwing a plate against the kitchen wall with all the force of his still-powerful pitching arm. Mili grabbed my hand in terror. My parents argued a lot, but it was usually Mami who broke things. When a man breaks something in anger, the next thing he grabs may be one of your limbs; we had heard that said by women in our own house. But Mami was sitting calmly with her *café* and Salems, watching impassively as the pink plate bounced off the wall and spun like a top on the floor of her kitchen. Papi picked it up and held it aloft for her to see.

"Unbreakable Pyrex, a space-age material. Dishes that won't ever have to be replaced." His words were so obviously rehearsed that I almost burst out laughing, but I noticed my mother's face was stern; this was old business between them: the American way versus the Puerto Rican way.

"And ugly as the original sin." My mother flicked the ashes of her cigarette into a pink saucer identical to the one Papi had thrown against the wall. She took a sip from a pink cup, obviously its mate. We knew then that her comment was a moot aesthetic judgment, since her sink was already full of floating pink tableware. From then on, we would be eating and drinking from our eternal china. Papi had come home with it one day, as proud of his purchase as if he had discovered Ponce de León's Fountain of Youth: today unbreakable dishes, tomorrow a cure for all the world's ills. Progress through American ingenuity was a rollercoaster ride that he was constantly preparing us to experience. So he took his brother's announcement of his and Patricio's imminent departure for Nueva York as welcome news, an advance guard to his own not-so-secret plan to move us to the mainland, at least for a while, so we could experience the twentieth century in all its power and glory. He would have to break it gently to Mami, who was attached to her family by multiple apron strings, dependent for her emotional stability on our bi-monthly visits to her mother's house, where she went to replenish her psyche, to refill her cup of fortitude. Mamá's casa was the source of the spiritual nourishment she needed to bear her personal cross. I imagined Mami's cross was made of pink Pyrex. But light or heavy, it was a woman's burden and her privilege to sacrifice her own needs and desires in order to one day reach that pinnacle of praise: *Se sacrificó por su familia.* It helped to have company in your misery, to have a group of female relatives with whom to compare your progress toward martyrdom, to share generational wisdom about babies and husbands, and to plot—for there is art to suffering. Power is a thing learned from others who have obtained it creatively and wielded it wisely.

A *CUENTO* AND THE SERENADE IN NINE INNINGS

Papi's Women

Perhaps because he seemed so sad and mysterious, my father was attractive to women. When my mother spoke of "the women" in my father's past, the word mujeres *took on every sinister connotation ever attached to the sex.* Tenía mujeres, *he had women, as if she were saying he had smallpox, but she stayed with him anyway, as was her duty. I remember those days best from my mental picture of a shirt that my mother hated and which my father often wore when he was going out by himself at night. It was of an uncharacteristic color, design, and texture, for when he was not in his work costume of blue coveralls, he usually wore the subtle uniform of Puerto Rican respectability, the white* guayaberas *and razor-creased black pants. This festive shirt that he put on for the* mujeres *was a flaming orange with gold threads running in a crisscross pattern down the front. It had to be ironed with care and precision. On those evenings, I would watch my mother slamming down the iron on the board, stretching the hated garment across it, keeping her eyes fixed to her task. She would press her lips together into a thin line as if to keep angry words or cries of pain from escaping. Once she had finished, she would carry the shirt by the collar and hang it on the back of a chair. He would pluck it off the chair without a word and take it to their room, where he would finish dressing. Then there would be the sound of my mother slamming the iron down almost simultaneously with the front door clicking shut.*

The Serenade in Nine Innings

It seems that my father had a dream as a young man—of having a song he wrote recorded. It was not a love song or a song about love betrayed, which is the prime topic of Puerto Rican popular music; it was instead a lyrical piece about the only activity that gave him pure joy: baseball. He had been, at eighteen, a star pitcher for his high-school team, but then he broke his ankle in a collision with another player. The song was a dirge, a mournful hymn to his moment of glory, too soon gone; a melody sent into space like a time capsule to preserve a moment. My father played a few chords on an old guitar and sang it to his compañeros at Chavo's cafeteria one afternoon while he rested his swollen foot on a shoeshine stool. It was fiesta week in the pueblo, so there were also many strangers present—itinerant musicians, who made the circuit of festivals around the island. Some of these men congratulated my father on his fine composition; in fact, it was their compliments that planted the seed of hope in his heart. For weeks, as he recuperated and courted my mother, he perfected the lyrics and set them to a simpler melody, one that reflected the feelings of yearning he had after meeting her. And she traded her heart for his song.

It was the week when they announced their engagement that he heard it—his song—played on the radio. Of course it had a different title—not "Serenade in Nine Innings," later to be referred to by him simply as "La Serenata," a title he had finally settled on after much thought. The rhythm had been speeded up so now it sounded more like a mambo rather than the bolero he had intended it to be. He had his friends listen to it, and they all agreed it was "Serenade" and it had been stolen! My father took a bus to the radio station in Ponce, pushed and harangued his way to the manager, who laughed in his face when he heard the story, dismissing him with "Go home and write another hit tune, son, and I'll believe you."

No one outside the pueblo ever believed him, of course. And he never tried writing another song, as far as I know. But for years, he noted how many times he heard the song played, computing in a series of ledgers how much money it had made for the thieves. In due time the story of his near brush with fame and fortune, the lost dream, became his cuento for life.

Mami suspected that Papi was seeing other women again. I heard them arguing fiercely behind their bedroom door, and now that I was one in solidarity with all suffering womankind, I began to try to find out for myself whether her suspicions were true.

I confided my fears about Papi to Patricio, who had turned into a man almost overnight. He had grown several inches and he shaved now. His face was blessed with an unblemished golden complexion—evidence of our fathers' European roots. My inheritance was more complex—similar features, but with my mother's darker skin tone topped by a head of coarse thick hair that Patricio liked to pile up in an outrageous bouffant. Now that we both had been transformed by puberty, we were not allowed to be alone much during the last few weeks before he and Tío left for New York. But I sneaked over whenever I could. Amazingly, Patricio was being very cooperative about the move. He finally told me his plan, after first having me swear on a stack of his dictionaries that I would not reveal it to anyone.

Patricio had adult *compañeros* now. Artists and university students whom he had met in Old San Juan. He told me about the cafés and cantinas where students from the university met to argue about politics and to talk about art and literature. I had no idea that this happened right in our own city. I had read about decadent Bohemian artists in the romantic *novelas* I borrowed from my mother's room. But they were all set in Spain, and everybody knew that Europe had tradition and culture; Puerto Rico only had fads and fashions, *la moda*. He said a friend had taken him to the meeting places where student artists made a little money by selling turista paintings at the park and the plaza, quickie art done in no time according to a surefire formula: scenes of pristine beaches, exotic flowers, big-breasted dancing girls in Mexican costumes, or portraits of robust brown women selling coconuts at roadside stands. Patricio said they had a great time coming up with ideas for these canvases. Their serious art was not much in demand. Many of these young men had begun turning to the Indian origins and the African roots of our island's culture and were developing a new style that had little to do with the chamber of commerce's depictions of Puerto Rico as *La Isla del Encanto*, the enchanting vacation island where the U.S. dollar was the common currency. But the turista art bought their groceries and paid their rent.

Patricio's face came alive as he told me about his new friends and how at home he felt with them.

"Then why do you want to leave?"

"I need to get away from Papi. We fight all the time, Consuelo. I think he hates me."

"But you're going with him."

Patricio smiled in a way that reminded me of my father when he told his cuentos. I was amazed at how much they resembled each other and how completely different they were.

"He is providing me with a ticket to freedom, Consuelito. He just doesn't know it."

"What about your friends here?" I resented Patricio's eagerness to leave our island—and me.

"My closest friend here will be in New York when I get there. He's got friends in the city, even a place to live, and an apartment he shares with other painters in Greenwich Village."

Patricio got the *Britannica* volume labeled N and showed me the photographs of a concrete city, much bigger than San Juan and almost uniformly gray in color. I told him that I found New York City ugly and depressing.

"These are only black-and-white photos, niña." Patricio laughed, but he knew what I meant.

The plan was for me to join the English club at school, which had a pen-pal program with students in the United States. At home, I would say I was in correspondence with an American student named Patty. Patricio would write to me under that name. I agreed to that arrangement, but it frightened me that it meant never revealing his whereabouts—for as soon as he arrived in New York and made contact with his friend, he planned to run away. I knew I would lose him to that other person. He was already far away from me in his mind, and this thought made me cry. Patricio held me like a baby and kissed my forehead.

"You're my darling niña, Consuelo. I will never forget you. You know that I cannot live with him any longer. But I will always be there for you, *mi amor*."

He rocked me in his arms until I stopped sobbing. Who would ever comfort me like this again?

When Patricio and Tío cleaned out their house and packed, I inherited my cousin's art supplies, his books on nature and poetry, and the chemistry set, which had once transformed the world for us. English had been our language for privacy, and by the time he left, I was very good at it: good enough to read all the books in his collection. They opened up a world so much bigger than the one I knew that I became addicted to their fantasies, the intoxicating trips to places that were mine alone to experience. I could read about topics my parents would find scandalous, and I could do it in front of them or out on the porch in full view of all the neighbors and no one would know. And so I learned to keep secrets the way Patricio had.

A few days before we were to drive Tío Domingo and Patricio to the airport, I decided to do something that was totally out of character. I told my cousin that I wanted to skip school one day and go into historic Old San Juan with him. At first he said no, arguing that if we got caught, I would be the one to get severely punished, as I would be violating several of the parental rules: cutting school, being out unescorted with a boy, going into San Juan without an adult, and, worse, being seen in the company of a certified troublemaker. I said I did not care. I wanted to see for myself the places he had described: the cafés, the artists having passionate discussions about their work, and the raucous university students who were in the news for their demonstrations on the famous Río Piedras campus.

"But niña, these people either go to classes during the day or they work. Most of them meet in the cafés after dark." Patricio's tone made me a little angry; he sounded patronizing, as if he could persuade me with weak arguments not to do something I had decided on without consulting him.

"I'll go by myself. I want to see San Juan without a chaperon. I just wanted your company, Patricio, but I know where the bus stop is, and tomorrow, after I drop Mili off at school, I'm going into the city."

I stormed out of his house without giving him a chance to speak. Something new was happening to me as I prepared myself to face life without my best friend. I was absorbing his spirit of rebellion, learning to use the creativity I had developed at his side to gain control of hours and, soon, of whole days of my life.

I had seen Patricio face the enemy and survive. The enemy was anyone who stood in your way when you knew with absolute certainty that you were doing what you had to do. I loved my sister, but I was tired of constantly watching out for her. I needed to think of myself for a while, to see what independence tasted like. In going to San Juan I'd get to see for myself the land's end of the island, the place where you either flew away toward the open sea and the unknown beyond, or turned back to the safety of known territory, where the way home was labeled in both kilometers and miles. Maybe I would have a better sense of my future when I looked away from the island.

Tensions at home were intensifying. Although no one actually said so, Mili's behavior was affecting each of us in a different way. Her growing strangeness was the secret we kept from ourselves. It would be a while before we came to understand the true meaning of the word *tragedia*.

Papi had suddenly become interested in clothes and Mami went through his side of the closet daily, checking pants pockets, inspecting shirt collars and the handkerchiefs she starched and ironed for the telltale signs of a woman's perfume or lipstick marks. I had gathered from listening to Tía Divina's pronouncements at my mother's kitchen table that men cheated as predictably as dogs mated, and, like the animals they resembled, they left a trail of smell and bodily fluids behind them. It was a source of horrified amazement to her that a woman, no matter how low, would want to service men when they did not have to.

I noticed my mother made no comment about the "servicing" part. But she asked many questions dealing with clues to a husband's infidelity, and the answers were given in the form of *cuentos de familia*, which Tía made new to fit every occasion. The stories she retold about cheating husbands had actually happened to women in the family, though she would often ask herself questions about crucial facts: "Was that cousin Sara Cristina's husband who took up with that *gorda*, that Pérez woman who weighs about three hundred pounds? Or was that Magaly's Raúl who is so skinny that everyone worried that *esa mujer* would smother him one day and leave his kids orphans?" Laughter. My mother glanced worriedly at me. I frowned back at her, letting her know I knew what was coming; I would be sent out of the room before the good part of the story.

"Niña, go see what Mili's doing, you know she shouldn't be alone all the time." I pointed to Mili sitting pensively on the swing that Papi had made. She was clearly within our view. Without interrupting Tía, who was hunched over her pink cup gathering her narrative power in a deep breath before she launched into *el cuento* about another *tragedia*, my mother pointed back to me and then outside. I pointed again to Mili and made an outline of a window. Mami pressed her lips together trying not to yell at me. I turned away from her so I could watch Mili while I listened to my aunt's story. My sister's lips were moving and she was staring off into the distance. Mami said young girls sometimes acted odd right before they started their periods. Maybe Mili was going to match Tía's old record for becoming a señorita early. A pudgy ten, she was already in a training bra, while I had hardly progressed much beyond mine.

Mami sighed as if resigned to letting me hear secrets about betrayals I surely would not need to know for a long while yet.

"Tía Josefa never has forgiven that *desgraciado* husband of hers." I wondered whether this was the same Tía Josefa who had eight or nine sons; so many that they had built her a new house in the country without having to hire anyone else to help. Abuela had noted this ruefully, of course, judiciously following her regretful statement by saying that, as for her, she was glad to have been blessed with three wonderful daughters and, *gracias a Dios*, no sons to give her headaches.

"Angélica, do you remember that *negrita* who lived at our grandmother's house and did some housework?"

"You mean Dama Lucinda?"

"The same one. Well, it was her she caught him with—*infraganti, m'hija*. Yes, Tío had been giving his best to the servant girl while courting the señorita. *Así son los hombres*."

"How did she find out about it?" Mami was interested in the "process" of infidelity. What were the signs? How did one discover the tracks leading to the bed of infamy?

"*Pues*, it's the smell mainly. You know they smell different, these women who will do anything with a man. They are not clean like decent women. And a man absorbs this smell. It gets on his cells, you know; his skin begins to absorb the odor of the other woman. After you sleep with a man you know what he should smell like, *verdad*?" My aunt laughed as she spoke of *el mal olor*, so we knew she must have been either joking or concealing something.

Mami looked at me. I was drinking my *café con leche* slowly, making it last through Tía's story. I avoided meeting her eyes.

"*Pero*, Divina, Tía Josefa had just married Tío. There must have been something that gave him away."

"Actually, it was the girl herself. She boasted about it to her friends around the pueblo. See, she and Josefa were the same age. They grew up together in Mamá's house, except that Dama Lucinda was the daughter of an old cook of grandmother's who died of tuberculosis when the girl was hardly more than a baby. Our grandfather hired a nurse for both of them, Josefa and Dama. Mamá says that her mother was furious about it. Imagine having your daughter and a servant's child being nursed by the same woman. But you know, back then a man's wishes were like God's commandments, and that is what the old man wanted. But that's another cuento." Tía's voice lowered to indicate a family "secret" was coming up. "I heard it said that Dama Lucinda was Abuelo's daughter by the cook." Tía Divina took a deep breath and picked up the thread of her main story with renewed passion.

"*Entonces*, when Abuelo had a stroke—from drinking too much Palo Viejo rum, Abuela made the girl Dama sleep on a pallet in the kitchen and do most of the housework. She could not stand the sight of the *mulatta*, but could not just throw her out, without the *malas lenguas* gossiping. You know how that is."

"Like *la Cenicienta*," I blurted out.

"Well, she was a proud *negra*, that one, not a humble Cinderella, niña. But she got her hands on the prince anyway." Tía winked at me, having obviously forgotten the moral of her story as she got caught up in the telling of it.

"So the girl talked about it, that's how Tía Josefa found out." Mami tried again to get the salient facts from her oldest sister, who was, after all, the living repository of their family's stories and wisdom. One just had to be patient with her circuitous storytelling style.

"It was her revenge, Angélica, don't you see? She and Josefa were the same age, grew up together in the same house, and may have been half-sisters, but Dama Lucinda was treated like a servant and slept on the kitchen floor while Josefa was given everything. So she seduced Tío, out of spite."

"*Bueno*," my mother said, meaning "that is that," not that anything was good. It was her way of imposing closure on a conversation.

The Studebaker soon pulled up into our gravel drive, and Papi and Tío came in the front door. Papi always took the visiting family males to the Golden Palms Hotel, where he gave them his maintenance engineer's tour of the most modern building on the island. But this pious Tío did not particularly enjoy being exposed to the earthly temptations he had recently given up, and he often returned anxious to collect his wife and head back to the pueblo in time for a revival at his church. This day the men looked upset.

"*¿Qué pasa?*" Both women spoke at once.

"The boy was there with Chachi."

"Patricio?" My mother turned to me. "Go tell Mili to come in and wash her hands. It's almost time to eat." This was a direct order, I could tell by the tone.

As I dragged myself out the back door, I heard Tío Yayo say in a furious whisper, "The *malditos* were splashing around in the swimming pool like two . . ." I could not make out the rest, but there were exclamations from the women of *"Dios mío"* and *"¡Está perdido!"*

Patricio was burning bridges before leaving the island. *Maldito y perdido*, damned and lost, they called him. But that was not really true. It made me sad to think that he was making sure that he would not return, but at the same time, his open rebellion excited me. He knew where he was going and he did not feel damned by his choices. He seemed thrilled to be breaking free from this place, flying away from this family with all its rules. And the way my father had spit out his own nephew's name told me there would be no turning back for my cousin. The rule most honored by a family is loyalty to one's blood, no matter what else they did. But it *did* matter what you did. Patricio Signe had stepped over the imaginary line. Now the family had someone else's *tragedia* on which to focus.

In the meantime, Mili was learning the language of birds.

"The little ones chase the big ones," she said to me when I caught her legs as she swung up, "they come too close to their nest." Then she asked, "Do you know what they say to each other all day, Consuelo?"

I tried to shake my head no, but Mili had caught my face between her sweaty palms. She pried my eyes open and made me look directly at her mouth. In an exaggerated way, like a language teacher enunciating foreign words, Mili told me what the birds said to each other: " 'Fly for your life.' Sometimes they repeat the word *volar* all day, Consuelito. *Volar, volar, volar, volar.* They keep saying it until one of them just can't stand it anymore and flaps his wings and is gone."

I said nothing, although Mili had buried her face in my neck. "Do you know why?" she asked. I could feel her mouth on my skin, near my jugular. Her were lips hot and wet, her teeth cool and sharp, as she said, "Because the sky is too blue, they can't see anything but *el azul, azul, azul,* and they get lost in it."

That night I began praying again. I prayed that there was a Guardian Angel as all the adults had assured us there would be, an angel holding our hands as we crossed the rickety bridge over the abyss. I prayed that such a benevolent creature was at my sister's side.

The day for my little excursion into Old San Juan with Patricio finally arrived. I was anxious to drop Mili off at her classroom door. But she dragged her feet and hesitated as if she wanted to tell me something. She waved good-bye instead when we both noticed that *La Señora*, as Mili called her fierce teacher, had her eagle eye on us. I watched my sister slink in with her head hung in an attitude of fear or humility that was totally out of character for her. I sensed trouble when I saw that La Señora Platasi was following Mili's progress toward her desk, keeping her eyes on her in a long and perhaps hostile stare that Mili did not acknowledge. My sister was more mature looking than her classmates; her weight had increased dramatically. She was not fat, but rather strangely voluptuous for her age. This year her grades had been dropping from her usual straight A's. My father blamed it on her teacher, claiming that it was this cranky woman's dislike of his lively pretty daughter that was the problem. It was his way of avoiding Mili's problems, to say that they were caused by other people's jealousy of her beauty and intelligence.

I decided to ask Mili about La Señora when I picked her up that afternoon. I headed for the bus stop instead of toward my school, a five-minute walk. I would have plenty of time to look around historic San Juan and get back before the last bell. Since I was a good student with a perfect attendance record, my teacher would accept my excuse of a sudden splitting headache like those I occasionally did get. I rarely let my headaches keep me from going to school, though. In fact, just getting out of the house often relieved the symptoms.

I got to the bus stop in time to see the fume-spitting bus round the corner, listing like an old ship. Because of the noise it made I did not hear Patricio until he was at my elbow, helping me board. He wasn't dressed in his usual khaki pants and white shirt. That day he was all in black: tight black chinos and T-shirt and movie-star sunglasses. I felt childishly silly in my blue plaid skirt and school-approved blouse with its Peter Pan collar and my brown loafers and socks.

We hugged after we settled into our seat at the back of the bus, giggling like happy co-conspirators. An old lady wearing a black mantilla as long as she was tall gave us a dirty look. Obviously, having just attended mass at the cathedral, her soul in a state of grace, she must have thought that Patricio and I were *novios*, a couple sneaking off on a school day to do who knows what behind our parents' backs. Patricio squeezed my elbow and we both laughed. I was nervous about my adventure but proud to be seen with a boy who looked like a matinee idol, a sexy rebel.

We soon left the suburban landscape of square cement houses and geometric neighborhoods behind and entered the winding cobblestone passageways of a city built in another century for another generation of Puerto Ricans who either walked or rode horses. The alleys were narrow and the hills steep. The bus dropped off its passengers at the edge of the street nearest the old town. When I stepped out onto the smooth cobblestones worn into reflective mirrors by centuries of feet, I could not help but stop to admire how they caught the intense blue sky.

For a while, we walked up and down hills on sidewalks so narrow we could not fit side by side. Patricio seemed to know where we were going so I remained quiet, taking it all in with this first breath of real freedom. I had visited Old San Juan before with my parents, but their narrated tours had interfered with my view. I did not want politics or history today; I wanted a little of the romance of Patricio's rebellion. At the center of the shopping area, where the street was lined with stucco buildings in pastel colors, with shops filled with tourist trash, we stopped to see a little square of blue ocean to the north: on the other side, the deeper blue of San Juan Bay was framed by the green mountains beyond.

"So, niña, what do you want to do? Do you want to tour El Morro Fort, *la fortaleza?*"

"I skipped school today, *primo*. I don't want to be educated at all for the next five or six hours." I took Patricio's arm and led him toward a bakery my nose had located in one of the little alleys. "First I want a cup of *café*, then I want to walk around for a while."

"As you wish, señorita." Patricio bowed in a theatrical way. Then he followed me toward the *repostería*. We both heard the long wolf whistle followed by catcalls in several voices at the same time. I turned around to see a group of men in work clothes staring and pointing at us.

"*¡Qué linda!*" one of them called out and the others laughed. "Looking good today, *mamita*."

I thought they were directing their comments at me, until I

saw Patricio's face. I pulled him into the little café with its own se-cluded courtyard. I quickly ordered coffee and guava *pastelillos* for us, and I kept my silence while Patricio breathed deeply, staring into his cup as if it held the future.

"Consuelo . . ." He shook his head and looked away as if telling himself to be quiet.

"Show me the places where you meet with the artists, Pa-tricio."

"They will not be there now." Patricio smiled sadly. "Those bums sleep late and come out like vampires at night."

"I don't care. I just want to go there with you."

"Okay, *mi amor*, your wishes are my commands today."

"And let's talk only in English, okay? I won't get to practice much when you leave."

"I'll write you letters in English, Consuelito. We'll practice that way."

"Patricio, let's talk now."

But a pall had settled over us like fog, and the brilliant blue sky could do nothing to dispel it. I began to understand that Patri-cio had chosen to keep his real life hidden from me. And all my ef-forts to know who my cousin really was had been in vain. Later I would understand that he had been afraid of saying the words that would define him, in any language.

La Señora handed me an envelope when I picked Mili up at the classroom door. It was addressed to my parents. Mili kept staring at it on the way home, not answering any of my questions. But she did not object when I carefully unfolded the note and read the three lines written in perfect penmanship. La Señora suspected Mili of emotional instability. She would like a conference with my parents at our home in order to discuss Mili's peculiar behavior.

"Have you been getting in trouble at school?"

"I fall asleep sometimes, Consuelito. And she doesn't let me play with my friends. That woman hates me. She wants to get me in trouble with Papi."

"Why Papi?"

"She says I've been playing bad games with boys."

"Why would she say that?"

"It's the *muchachos* who lie about me, Consuelito. Please don't let her talk to Papi." Mili held my hand so tight I thought she would break it. I saw the wildness in her eyes, but I knew I could not lie to her. This meeting had to happen. There were questions that had to be answered.

My heart was beating fast as I asked her the last question before we arrived at our front door.

"What *muchachos* are you talking about, Mili? Has somebody bothered you?"

But she did not answer. Instead, she turned her gaze inward as she did sometimes in church or while adults were talking around her. I had recognized this as her way of escaping, and I figured she went into her own thoughts as I did into mine when the world was just not interesting enough to stay tuned. But Mili's fugues were becoming a source of worry to my parents, who often had to call her name several times before getting a response. Yet there were moments when she was the same lively girl, giggly and full of such energy that we would end up wishing that she would be quiet and give us all a rest.

Mami was at Tío Domingo's that afternoon, cleaning the house for her brother-in-law so he could start showing it to prospective buyers. I saw that Patricio was in his room because his window blinds were open. But I knew that his door would be locked. He no longer spoke to my parents. I put the teacher's note under Mami's ashtray with the Golden Palms Hotel design on it.

She would find it there as soon as she came in to have her hourly cigarette. I went out to the swing, a favorite place of Mili's, and as I turned my eyes toward the piece of sky visible through the thick branches of our mango tree, I tried to see what she saw. Concentrating hard on the blue space like I had seen her do, I could imagine shapes and colors I had not seen before. My sister was not sick or crazy. Papi was right, that woman was just simply jealous of our pretty Mili.

But what worried me had not been in the note. *Los muchachos*. What boys or men was Mili referring to? And why hadn't she complained at home that someone was bothering her? The image of Néstor with her at the fair came to me as a sharp pain in my head. I recalled the panic I had felt when I could not see Mili, and the revulsion when I saw his hands on her. I shook the thought away. That was behind us now. There was no need to dwell on it. Besides, I had boy problems of my own to think about.

I could not stop thinking of an older boy at my high school; a basketball player named Wilhelm Lugar, who had been born in Germany while his father was stationed there with the army. His elongated body fascinated me as I watched him practice on the afternoons when the English club met on one side of the gym. His skin was like polished mahogany and his fingers were long, elegant, and graceful as he flicked the ball from the wrist in a perfect arch—so that it found its way into the basket almost every time. When he was on the court I could barely concentrate on the conversation our English club was practicing. One time the ball had rolled toward our group, and in two strides of his long legs he was at my knees recovering it.

"Sorry," he said in English, "I didn't mean to interrupt."

The girls in our group giggled and my friend Marisa Morales elbowed me. I had been startled by Wilhelm's voice, which was low and soft and musical. His pronunciation was perfect, as our sponsor, Mrs. Rivera, pointed out to us. But he had grown up in the United States and on army bases in Europe, so that explained it. Marisa suggested to our earnest young teacher that we ask him to come tell us about his travels for one of our special programs. He would speak in English. It would be an educational experience. Marisa pinched my arm as she spoke. Mrs. Rivera said that was an excellent idea and she would speak to Coach Jimmy Santiago about it. From then on, for the rest of the day, it was as if I were in a dream of Wilhelm. I thought of him constantly, engaging in imaginary conversations where I spoke with him in perfect English.

My daydream was interrupted when my mother walked into the house. I jumped off the swing and headed over to Patricio's. I knew Mami would find the note and begin to question Mili, and I needed a little time before *my* interrogation began. I ran my fingers over the blinds outside Patricio's room in our secret code. I knew this was one of the last times I could count on taking refuge with him. He let me into a nearly empty space; everything he wanted to take with him had already been packed into two suitcases. There were boxes marked with my name. Others were still untaped and marked as either trash or church donation.

"My mother's things," Patricio explained when he saw me glancing at the open boxes. "I have to do something with them. My father would just set them all out on the sidewalk to be picked up by the garbage truck. I am taking all the clothes to the church, also her kitchen stuff. But I'm throwing out the *novelas* and women's magazines."

"Can I look through them?"

"Sure, Consuelito, take what you want. But there are better books to read than those." He pointed to a sealed box with my name on it.

I opened it in my room while I waited to hear my mother's strained voice call out my name. Through my open door, I could see that she had Mili sitting across the kitchen table from her. I heard, "Either you tell me or you tell your father when he gets home tonight." But my sister's beatific expression did not change with the rising threat in our mother's voice. It was as if she were sitting in frozen serenity like the Pietà, who, even with her dead son draped over her lap, managed to exude an eerie calm. I closed my door and left them in this strange tableau, a scene that stayed with me like a recurring dream, whose meaning will both haunt and forever elude you.

Patricio's box held one third of the *Encyclopaedia Britannica*. In the next few days I would drag the other two thirds of mankind's accumulated knowledge home; and I would spend the entire summer after Patricio left reading the books from A to Z, so that by the time Wilhelm spoke to me about living in Munich and Milan, I had already learned about some important things that started with the letter *M*. But it would be a long time before I reached the letter *T*, as in the word *tragedia*.

SILENCIO: The Lessons of the Forest

The childhood festival of the imagination that had been my years with Patricio ended on the day we packed into my father's Studebaker and took him and Tío to the airport. The ride was a quiet one with the three adults in the front seat talking in low tones about Tío's plans and expectations in Nueva York, and Patricio, Mili, and me sweltering in the backseat. I held Patricio's hand the whole time. Apparently, from the few words I could hear above the engine's roar and the traffic, my uncle had already made business contacts in Nueva York and Nueva Jersey and was encouraging Papi to consider a move. The island was too small for a man with ambition, he said, listing the problems of living in a place governed by an idealistic poet, Muñoz Marín, who had yet to come through for the small independent businessman like himself. I saw my mother square her shoulders and move almost imperceptibly away from her brother-in-law, though there was hardly any room to do so in the crammed front seat.

Patricio looked out the window the entire time, maybe saying good-bye to the San Juan architecture he knew so well. The day we had spent in the old city he had told me the history of the oldest buildings, including Juan Ponce de León's house, which still contained the little throne where the dreamer had planned to receive visitors before he was distracted by his quest for the Fountain of Youth. He never saw his house finished. Patricio told me that he read poetry before visiting the old places because it was the poets who had the right words to describe beauty in the world. I had found the poems of a woman named Julia de Burgos among the encyclopedia volumes he had given me, but I had not read them yet. Poetry still frightened me a little, with its mysteries hidden between the lines; I preferred facts I could collect and memorize, everything as well documented as possible. Mili looked out the other window, her curly black hair blowing around her face.

At home there was a still unresolved *situación muy seria* concerning my sister. I got to sit in during the conference between my parents and Mili's teacher, La Señora Platasi, held at our kitchen table. The meeting had revealed one thing to Papi and another to Mami, points they argued over at every occasion. Mili stood accused of inattention in class, of pretending not to respond to her teacher even when addressed directly and of lying about it later. In her own defense, she insisted that there was so much noise around her that she could not hear her teacher.

"What noise?" various adults had asked her.

The mice under the floor squeaking, she said, or the wind shaking the leaves on the trees, and especially the birds singing the same song over and over until she wanted to plug her ears. Sometimes she heard voices. What did the voices say? Bad things she would not repeat, Mili insisted. Besides Mili's ridiculous stories, the teacher also suspected my sister of inappropriate behavior, *"touching games with older boys"* is what she called it. She had no evidence of this except the snitching of other students and her own intuition.

During La Señora Platasi's obviously prepared indictment of Mili, my mother had briefly covered her face with her hands. Then she looked down at her hands tightly folded in her lap the rest of the time. I could see that she was fighting angry tears. My father got furious at the second allegation, ignoring the first as prejudice by her classmates against Mili for her popularity among older students. Mami was in tears when Mili's teacher left, shamed by the arrogant woman's suspicions of her younger daughter's morality. I had been admonished to keep an eye on Mili, as if I didn't already watch her almost more than they did, and to report anything she revealed to me. I was not about to betray my sister. Instead I kept my silence and observed her closely, mainly because I felt somehow responsible for her problems.

Yet Mili seemed less troubled by her circumstances than the rest of us. She rarely spoke to me either about real life or about her inner life. Mili's focus these days was on the lives of movie and TV stars whom she read about in the fan magazines. She watched TV every minute she could and spent whatever money she had on going to the *cine*. She spoke of the actors whose lives she followed on and off screen as if they were her friends and family.

"When I danced on television in *El Show Musical*," she announced at the table one day, "the singer—you know the boy who wears the shirts with sleeves that look like skirts with crinolines—kissed me on the mouth, and said my tongue could learn to sing . . ." But her soliloquy was often stopped by our father's nervous laughter. He would cut in with his own fantasy about our beautiful Mili.

Papi encouraged her to think of herself as a future beauty queen. Puerto Rico was, after all, famous for its beautiful women, and has always been represented in international competitions right along with the United States. It was one of the few areas where the island was given a separate status as a nation. But lately, Mili's upbringing, and their individual roles in it, had been subjected to kind of desperate scrutiny by my parents. Who was at fault for her *problema*? Mami angrily accused Papi of encouraging my sister to fantasize about a life to which she couldn't really aspire. That was why, Mami claimed, she didn't concentrate on school, always daydreaming about beauty contests and other frivolous pursuits. What she needed was a Catholic school education and to become *más seria* like me. Papi insisted that it was a mother's duty to shape a daughter's character—a woman's job. Their arguments were becoming more bitter each day, as their desperation over my sister's retreat from reality grew more serious and more obvious.

The Pan American gate where we waited for the flight from San Juan to Idlewild was as crowded and noisy as a family fiesta. The same flight left the island at three every afternoon with some one hundred Puerto Ricans on it heading for the gray city I had seen on the pages of my books. I imagined that the brilliant blue sky over the Atlantic Ocean would begin to darken as the airplane counted down the sixteen hundred miles toward the U.S. mainland, primary colors fading to steel gray like they did in a Technicolor movie as it ended. I looked at my cousin's face to see if he was showing any hesitation or anxiety, but his jaw was set like my father's when he was angry or determined to do something, like starting the Studebaker when it stalled at a light. Patricio was moving in only one direction now, and it was away from me. I believed that he would forget me as soon as he stepped off the airbus at eight that night and entered another world. I had memorized all the facts of the journey as I had learned to do with most things in my life. Knowing exactly what was happening, or was likely to happen, gave me a secret surge of power. No surprises if they could be avoided, not for me.

This resolution gave me license to eavesdrop and to spy on people whose plans and plots might affect me. For instance, through Patricio, who had asked Chachi, I knew my father was seeing a woman at the Golden Palms. She was a bartender and would-be salsa singer looking for a record contract. She sang for free at various dives around San Juan, hoping to be discovered. Marvela, as the former María González now called herself, believed that she only needed to record the right song to attain her dream of fame. Chachi thought she was using Papi for money to support a couple of her many bad habits. I walked around with my chest and head heavy with the burden of my knowledge. Did everyone lead a secret life?

When the adults had gone to get coffee, Patricio handed me a piece of paper.

"Here is your pen pal's address, niña. Don't forget to write."

"How soon are you going to be there?" I had imagined his plan would take weeks to put into effect. After all, it involved running away from home in a new place. What about money? How was he going to survive?

"My friend is already there. Every little detail has been worked out. Don't worry about me, Consuelito. We will meet again. I will always let you know where I am."

I lost control of my pent-up grief then and began crying on his shoulder. He held me gently in his arms like he always did when I needed to be babied, rocking me a little. I didn't see Mami until I felt her long nails digging into my arm. She pulled me away from Patricio.

"Quit acting like a child, Consuelo. Where is Mili?"

————

I saw Patricio handing over his ticket at the counter. I wanted to call out his name, say a proper *adiós*, but my mother was holding on to my arm, muttering something about Mili. I saw Patricio get in line to board his flight. He did not look back.

On the ride home Mami made a hand-washing motion about the departure of "that poor man Domingo and his sick son." She was ready to speak her closing *bueno* on their part in our life as a family. She could now concentrate on Mili's troubles and on her detective work on my father. She believed she didn't have to worry about me. I had been transformed in her mind into the good daughter, her indispensable ally. God had given her *una hija buena* to lighten the load of her cross. She was counting on my sense of *el sacrificio*: as a woman, it was to be my privilege and my burden. I began to experience a sense of dislocation when she talked about me this way, as if she were making up a cuento about someone else, some other girl named Consuelo.

CUENTOS FOR LA LUCHA

For support and ammunition in her good fight, Mami went to Abuela's house often. There, the living library of a woman's reference volume on life could be tapped. Until now, all she had had to do was ask Abuela or one of her sisters; someone would always have an answer, or at least words of comfort. All she needed to know to help her daughter and to save her husband from the trashy mujeres *could be found in her own mother's and her sisters' collected experiences and family cuentos. Abuela had an "on" button that started automatically at the mention of certain subjects. She would then dispense advice stamped with the sacred seal of her mother's wisdom. What Abuela's mother, the matriarch Isadora, had said and done during her lifetime was indelibly etched in my grandmother's mind as wisdom. It was hard to dispute it because* the woman had been a phenomenon in her time. A seamstress of national acclaim who had sewn clothes for the high and mighty, including the vestments of the bishop of Puerto Rico himself.

More extraordinary than her golden needle was that she had opened a shop and sewing school where several generations of highly skilled seamstresses had been trained. Of course, all this was now lore since the women's thread industry had practically vanished from our island—most of the trained women having emigrated to the United States during the thirties and forties. It was a real tragedia, I heard said at least a thousand times, that the same women who cut, sewed, and embroidered works of art under Mamá Isadora's wise tutelage were now working in dark factories where the noise from the monstrous machines did not allow the discussion that is necessary for learning and creating. Yet Mamá Isadora had left a legacy of wisdom that would last at least partially through one more generation in my family. Her parables for a woman's life had been absorbed by her daughter and granddaughters, and now I was being indoctrinated into a new Gospel According to Isadora edited for my generation.

One morning, six months after Patricio went to New York, we left San Juan especially early. On our trip to Abuela's, Papi wanted to show us a new observatory being built by the American scientists and engineers to listen for signals from outer space. Mami agreed to his plan if we could stop by the rain forest, El Yunque. It was one of her favorite places on this side of the island, with its primeval forest of gnarled trees and thick emerald-green vegetation, its veil of mist. One could stand in the middle of a cloud at the summit. The chorus of birds and frogs all singing at once made her feel like she was in another place, out of time, close to when the island was inhabited only by a few Indians, she had once said. I knew what she meant. The island had its own voice, but it was growing fainter, drowned out by car and machine noises, and by too many people living too close together.

When we were in the forest Papi always held us in a tight little group, as if one of us were going to vanish suddenly into the fog.

"I can fly from here!" Mili cried out suddenly as we got to the observation deck of El Yunque. We all laughed at her passionate outburst, but being closest to her, I could see that she had what looked like tears running down her cheeks. Her smile convinced me that it was probably mist, however, the same condensation that was puffing my hair into a mossy cloud.

"Too much noise here for a supposedly peaceful place," Papi observed. His tone was ironic because Mami had fallen into her rain-forest meditative mood.

"Not *enough* noise," she finally said.

"What do you mean, Angélica? Should they play some mambos over loudspeakers for the birds and the tourists?"

Ignoring his sarcastic challenge, Mami said in a sad whisper, "I read somewhere that the parrots are dying off. You don't hear them so much anymore. And you almost never see them in flocks like you used to a few years ago."

"And who is killing the *cotorra puertorriqueña*?" Papi chuckled.

Mami gave him a disdainful glance. "Maybe the Martians you believe are out there. Now that they've been invited to our island by the American scientists, they've decided to eat the Puerto Rican parrot first, then maybe us."

"Very funny, Angélica. You're nearly as funny as your father on the subject of *los americanos*."

"I should be as smart as that old man." My mother was worked up now and I knew the educational tour was over. I took one last long look through the scenic viewer that Mili had hogged until the dime's worth of looking was almost over. I saw right where my world ended, but not where Patricio's began, a thousand miles away.

When we finally arrived at the pueblo, Abuela sent Mili and me out to the chicken yard to choose a fat bird for dinner. I knew she and Mami were going to hold a high-level conference in her room, and I felt slightly offended that my status as señorita and almost their equal was being ignored. I wanted to hear Abuela say what Mamá Isadora would have done if she had had to face Mami's dilemmas. Even after death Mamá Isadora was still solving problems for the living. What she had spoken was like great poetry or prophecy—it could be interpreted as needed.

I grabbed the nearest feathered thing and handed it to Mili. She petted it and spoke to it in words I could not quite hear or understand, but I encouraged her to sit in the hammock Abuela had hung between two trees with the petrified bird on her lap. I went to the window of Abuela's room, where the blinds were always kept slightly cracked for air but never wide open to the damaging heat of the sun. I pretended to be fascinated by the smelly herbs she had planted in the shady moist spot. The one I picked up to bring to my nose happened to stink like foot rot or something equally disgusting. I threw it as far away from me as I could, but the odor had penetrated my skin. I'd have to scrub my hands with Abuelo's pumice soap later.

Crouching under the window I could hear the two women clearly. I imagined them sitting on the spacious bed in the room decorated like a family museum. A portrait of the matriarchal Doña Isadora dominated one wall. She had been a thin woman with large liquid eyes that were the only tender feature on a severe face. The stern expression may have been put on for the occasion of the photograph, since one of the legendary qualities of my great-grandmother had been her loquaciousness and sense of humor. It was said that she could talk nonstop to her apprentices for the entire ten-hour day she kept her shop open. No wonder they had been able to glean so much wisdom from the woman. If she had talked ten hours a day for the twenty-five years she was in business, she was bound to have said a few interesting things just in terms of numerical odds.

"Young girls go through many changes as nature transforms them into women." Abuela was in her high-diction mode, as if the rhetorical prowess of her dead mother entered her from beyond the grave when someone needed her advice. "Some girls have even fallen prey to seizures which disappear after their menstrual cycle begins."

"I've heard of those *ataques* in girls. Didn't Divina have a few when Papá refused to let her see that boy, what was his name, the son of that policeman?"

"Your sister did get sick like that once, but she was older, fifteen. I don't think it had to do with the Martínez Prado boy. Your father did the right thing when he said no to that relationship. *Ese muchacho* wasn't right for Divina."

Abuela seemed to have gotten derailed by a new train of thought, but my mother's next question ended the discussion about her middle sister's broken romance of twenty years ago: "He was black. That's why Papá didn't want him for Divina, right?"

"That is not true, Angélica. We are not racists in this house!" Abuela's angry tone would silence Mami, I knew; she didn't want to provoke Abuela's wrath and risk being shut out of family business for weeks on end.

"He has never married," Mami ventured in a timid tone.

"That's been his only act of kindness toward women." Abuela laughed.

"About Mili." Mami knew to veer away from the precipice when it concerned Abuela.

"Mili needs you to show her the way, *hija*. Spend time with her; teach her how to live a creative life." Abuela resumed her role as oracle.

"Creative. How? I am not an artist. I don't know how to do anything artistic. Besides, Mili uses her imagination a little too much already."

"Angélica, you forget that being creative, like your abuela Isadora—may her blessed soul rest in eternal peace—always said, is a matter of doing one or two things very well. I taught you how to embroider, how to crochet. I told you how a woman could plan her days and her whole life; how she can pray for the living and the dead while her hands are busy. Teach your daughter how to go inside herself and find her identity as a woman."

"I'll try, Mamá. Mili is not like Consuelo. She doesn't listen for very long. *¡Ay Dios mío!* What if there is something wrong with her mind? What if she's sick?" I heard the anguish in my mother's voice.

"I do not believe she is *loca*." Abuela clapped her hands hard as if to keep my mother's attention focused on her words, or perhaps to keep her from falling into despair. "No, we have no insanity in our family. At least not on my side. In your father's family there have been a few *Independentistas*, though."

The tension was relieved with laughter. I was getting a cramp from my spying position and as I stretched up I heard the beginning of the discussion about Papi. Mami was presenting the list of clues to his infidelity that she had been gathering for a year, starting with his interest in clothes and his gift giving. I could imagine Abuela nodding in agreement. Yes, these were clear signs of trouble.

At that moment there was a commotion in the direction of the chicken yard. I had forgotten about Mili. I turned around and what I saw horrified me. Even now I can vividly recall the gory scene: my sister covered in blood, holding a huge knife in her hand. I ran to her, screaming her name. She was laughing and waving the knife around. And at her feet was the fat white hen she had been cuddling only moments before, its neck dangling by a string of flesh, feathers soaked pink.

"What did you do?" I grabbed Mili's hand and pried the knife away from her, slicing the knuckle of my index finger as I did.

"Consuelito, I did it! Just like Abuelo does. I got the hen ready for dinner!"

"*¡Dios mío!*" Mami came running out the back door followed by Abuela. What she must have seen was right out of a horror movie. Both her daughters covered in blood, her "good daughter" holding a dripping butcher knife in a hand that was gushing blood. But it was the happy smile on Mili's face that must have been the most frightening sight of all.

It was my grandfather who, in his usual direct manner, brought up the unpleasant fact of my paternal grandmother's unfortunate propensity to go crazy.

"In those days all a husband could do was keep her locked up in the house until it passed." Abuelo shook his head in the direction of the bathroom, where Mili was showering and Mami was soaking the bloody dress.

I had changed into my dungarees and T-shirt even before allowing Abuela to bandage my finger. She had sniffed in disgust, telling me that I smelled like *flores de muertos*, cloyingly sweet like a funeral wreath. Abuelo had wandered in during the commotion. I sat across from him at the little table in his library. I was still trembling, unable to think of anything but the sight of Mili holding the bloody knife and the sound of her crazy laughter. I listened to what the old man said, trying to make him keep his voice down so that Abuela wouldn't come and put an end to his dredging up of bad memories; not something she allowed in her house unless *she* initiated it for educational purposes. Morality tales were acceptable, even if they were unpleasant true family stories; the recounting of past troubles and tragedies, however—not good for the children to hear.

But Abuelo liked a good story, whatever the source, and the best usually involved mayhem of some kind. This one was about relatives I had not known. Both my paternal grandparents had died during an influenza epidemic when I was too little to remember. All I had were pictures of a dark woman with braids circling her head like a black halo above a mournful face. Mili had the same shape of mouth as my dead Mamá Clara Consuelo, after whom I had been named, and the same round face, though my sister's expression was so much more animated than the one in the photo that the resemblance seemed merely coincidental.

"It was a real *tragedia,* niña. The woman would change completely when it happened. It was as if a demon entered her body for the time it lasted. Then she would go back to her old self, a quiet decent woman, very pious. But always sad, *muy triste.*"

"What did she do when she went . . . when she changed, Abuelo?" I whispered to let him know that he should keep his lector's voice low. But he raised himself up in his chair, his index finger shooting up in the air, and he thundered: "It was not spoken about in decent company, *hija.* But Clara Consuelo went after men when she got sick. It was *muy trágico* for your father and your Tío Domingo. And as for your grandfather, he was humiliated beyond words. But the people of our pueblo all helped him as best we could, since her *familia* was in San Juan and had to be sent for when it happened. Someone, usually the man she accosted, would bring her home, and Don Carlos would lock her in her room until it passed."

"¡Señor!" My grandmother spoke in such a stern voice that both of us jumped. "This child has had enough trouble today. May I see you in my room for a moment?"

Abuelo gathered his dignity, picked up the hat that had leaped from his hand, and, nodding gravely to me, followed his wife to her inner chamber where he would get her lecture on the damaging effect of bad memories on children—the Gospel According to Mamá Isadora.

CONSOLAR: To Console, to Comfort

The next day we packed the car and took the *autopista* back home. My parents looked straight ahead and did not speak. Mili was still staying at Abuela's. Papi had not liked the idea of leaving my sister, but Mami had given him a look that meant: *We will talk when we get home.* He had assented so humbly that I had assumed he thought Mili had started bleeding. He said, "I understand," when he meant, *I don't want to know any more about it.* Mami had responded with a curt, "No you don't, Carlos. You don't understand."

I was frightened for Mili. More and more she seemed out of touch, trapped in her own inner world, showing little interest in her surroundings or in people. I now suspected that it, whatever "it" was that had been slowly transforming her, was out of control.

At home my mother talked obsessively about Mili slaughtering the chicken. My father responded with a forced smile. He would have preferred to forget it. He tried to enlist me in making it a joke.

"And she said that she was getting it ready for dinner, huh Consuelito?"

Mami stared at him in disbelief through a cloud of cigarette smoke. "You don't think it's strange for a little girl to kill an animal with a butcher knife, Carlos?"

"Didn't you help your mother slaughter hens all the time, Angélica? It was going to happen anyway. I don't know why you're trying to make this into something that it isn't. Mili is almost a señorita. You keep saying that yourself. She's adventurous . . ."

"She should have *aventuras* like her papi?"

The word *aventuras*, the way Mami said it, infuriated him. He knew what she meant. Papi rose from the table, crushing and twisting his cigarette into the ashtray as though he were trying to make sure it was dead.

I finished washing the unbreakable dishes that I had been lingering over, and left the kitchen before Mami thought of a reason to make me go.

I heard their argument all the way in my room.

By this time, my second year of high school was well under way and, to escape the melodrama at home, I was developing my first intense involvements outside *la familia*. Wilhelm Lugar had offered to tutor me in English after we had formally met at his presentation to our English club. He had shown slides of all the European and American cities where he and his family had lived, and I had had the chance to show off my knowledge of facts about those places—up to the letter *M* that is. He had laughed after class when I told him why I had not commented on Paris or Palermo. He said he looked forward to talking with me after I got past the *S*'s, as in *sexy*, in the *Britannica*. I took it as an invitation to meet again.

———————

I hoped that Mili would somehow miraculously snap out of her strange condition and that my family would finally focus on my *quinceañera*, when I would turn fifteen. I felt alone with my fears. I needed someone other than my parents to confide in. I missed Patricio desperately. He would have known how to think about this, and he would have comforted me at a time when our family was closing around Mili's secret as if it were a monster growing in her belly that we all had to deny. But more than six months had passed, and Patricio, using the name Patty Swan, had sent me only one brief note.

Then the bad news arrived by telegram: Patricio was missing. Tío Domingo thought his son might try to return to the island. My parents were to report Patricio to the police as a runaway and a thief.

The same day I got a letter from Patty Swan.

My dear Consuelo,
I sincerely hope that this letter will be in your hands before "all hell breaks loose"—an American expression you should learn. When my father discovers that I have left home he will make trouble for everyone. It took me longer than I anticipated to plan my escape. It has been very hard, *mi niña*; I have been lonely for you and for my friends on the island. But this city is not as dark and depressing as you might imagine. It's got the most beautiful buildings I have ever seen, and museums filled with art, libraries with millions of books, and, best of all, lots of places to hide. Someday, Consuelito, you will visit me here, and I will show you things that will amaze you. Do not worry about my father's threats. I am of legal age and I have committed no

crimes. The money I used to get away was mine, from some sketches I sold. Soon I will send you a drawing I know you will like. How does it feel to be almost fifteen? I wish I were there to attend your birthday. You are a *mujercita* now, as our dear relatives will say.

It might be best if you destroy my letters since your parents may recognize my handwriting. My friend addresses the envelopes for me. Remember: I'll always let you know where I am, but you must never reveal my whereabouts to anyone. I will carry your image in my mind wherever I go, *mi amor.*

Love,
Patty

I could see the old Patricio between the lines even as a new self-confident Patricio emerged. I didn't want him to distance himself from me as he had with the rest of our family. So I continued to write to him.

My letters to Patricio became a journal for me, into which I poured my most intimate thoughts. But it was as if I were sending them into the void, since I could not really think of the strange cold place where he had vanished as real. It was more like writing to myself, though I addressed the envelopes to Patty Swan and dropped them into mailboxes on my way to school.

My concerns about Mili were not to be shared outside the family. It was considered betrayal by both my parents to talk about our personal matters with others, although I heard the adults in my family discussing the most intimate aspects of other people's lives with great relish. Besides, I didn't want to talk about Mili as my birthday approached. It was Wilhelm who was on my mind. I watched him play basketball while I carried my love like a rare jewel. I didn't want to share it with anyone, though some of my schoolmates thought they knew something. They must have seen us lock eyes often enough during the day. At games, I sat as close to the court as I could, and during warm-ups he managed to swing his sleek body past the bleachers with the obvious intent of impressing me. I gave myself over to the almost dizzying pleasure of the sight of his dark brown skin glistening with sweat, his long limbs corded with muscles, and his face like a carved African mask with a little Indian slant to his golden brown eyes. As I watched him jump high above the other players, tilting his whole body in midair, I held my breath, halfway expecting him to float or fly over all of us in that gymnasium. Marisa would sometimes poke me in the ribs to remind me to take a breath before I fainted.

So it was no surprise that I responded with my whole being to Wilhelm's note asking me to wait for him alone after the game. I was nearly sick with excitement as I waited with Marisa, who had agreed to disappear after we passed the danger zone of vigilant teachers.

"*Boba,*" Marisa whispered in my ear, "don't be a sissy. This is what you've been waiting for, right?" I nodded, feeling both anticipation and fear; fear that Wilhelm would now discover what a dull person I really was. Had I given him the idea that I was like some of the girls who went out with the basketball players, then boasted about their sexual adventures? My gaze had certainly held promises. But even I didn't know what I was willing to do with him. Nothing and no one in my life had ever made me feel like this: hungry and full at the same time.

"Papito says that Wilhelm *está enamorado de ti*. He's in love with you, Consuelito. But he's shy about talking to you because his Spanish is not too good." Marisa reported everything that she could pump out of her brother about Wilhelm. It was true that he spoke Spanish like I spoke English, with hesitation. Having been a military brat, Wilhelm had spoken Spanish only at home with his mother. Now he was doing badly in his regular classes. Only his basketball-star status kept him from being shunned by the other students.

I squeezed Marisa's hand when I saw Wilhelm emerge from the locker room, a head taller than his teammates, smiling at all the compliments on his game, quietly accepting the rowdy praise with nods of his head; but his eyes were on me, on *me*.

We walked with Marisa until we were outside school territory. As agreed, she left us a few blocks from my home. But I soon forgot all about her and the rest of the world. It was one of those early evenings in San Juan when the breeze brings a taste of the ocean to your mouth. It is a gift, my mother said once when I complained that the salt made my eyes water: no other place on the island was lucky enough to have the air purified by the sea. I had relegated that remark to my mother's romantic nature, but as I walked next to Wilhelm, I reconsidered her words. There *was* something in the air that made my skin tingle and my eyes grow moist; it carried the promise of adventure, and that night I liked the feeling.

Wilhelm, who had been mostly quiet, even when Marisa had rattled on about how much she admired his game, started to say something in Spanish, then hesitated, embarrassed that he couldn't think of the word he needed. I offered to speak in English with him, if he didn't laugh at my pronunciation. He took my hand in his as if it were the most natural thing in the world, smiling his gratitude. I was glad that it had gotten dark as we approached my neighborhood. The gossips would be inside watching their after-dinner *telenovelas*. I listened intently as Wilhelm told me about the lonely gypsy life of the military brat. I was amazed that someone as interesting as he was could feel alienated.

I was the one who pulled him toward a vacant lot next to Señora Sereno's house, where the trees and bushes had not been cleared for construction yet. I had to stand on my toes to reach his mouth, and it was like tasting the fruit of knowledge, knowledge of good and evil: a nearly ripe pomegranate, the heart-apple. Bitter. Sweet. Familiar and strange. A consolation. And I knew instantly that I wanted more.

LA FAMILIA: A Crown of Thorns and Roses

It was the late fifties and life on the island was changing fast. My cousins and I were speaking a language that separated our world from that of our parents; we had invented a new way to describe our world, a slang peppered with terms like "rock-and-roll" that had no direct equivalent in our native tongue. This bothered our mothers less than the clothes we insisted on wearing, both boys and girls in blue *mahones*—the workingman's dungarees—men's shirts, and loafers. This fashion was followed mainly in San Juan, the big city. In Abuela's pueblo the priest still decreed women's fashion from his pulpit on Sunday. He would not let a woman attend mass if her shoulders were bare or her knees showed. He once stopped a wedding because the bride showed too much flesh, and he asked for the shawl of an old lady who was covered in black from head to foot. The poor girl had to go through the ceremony wearing an old lady's camphor-scented black shawl over her costly wedding gown. Abuela had made her hand-washing gesture when she told this cuento: "The bride knew the rules, she could have waited a little to expose her body before God and man."

To the women in my family, it was not merely a matter of modesty—the clothes you wore marked you immediately as either *gente educada* or *jíbaros*. If anyone's child could wear the same clothes, class distinctions would be blurred. Being well dressed meant a lot to these women, especially since we were not exactly upper-class, not even really quite middle-class like the lawyer's family or the other upper crust of the pueblo. We had been raised from dreaded lower-class status only by Mamá Isadora's genius. A farmer's widow with children still at home, my great-grandmother had managed to build enough capital so that her daughter never had to work for others. Unfortunately, my abuela had married a man for his mind and good looks who had failed to add to the family coffers. Nevertheless we were not *polilla*, the common urbanized peasants, who, like termites, were to be found wherever they could build their messy nests and procreate. La polilla. They were easily identifiable by their cheap clothes and shoes, their bad manners, and for having children frequently and indiscriminately. This, anyway, was cultural history according to the women of our family.

Our parents worried that *la gente decente*, like us, were becoming overrun by the polilla. They were vigilant about anything in our appearance or behavior that might indicate a regression to the lower social strata. We could become polilla by acquiring their bad habits and lapsing in our devotion to the Catholic Church. An era was ending on the island: Spanish colonial customs were fading into the background as American culture saturated the airwaves.

I felt it at home too. Mamá Isadora's old recipes for domestic bliss would not work for me. But Mami was a believer, even though Mili's behavior had defeated Abuela, with all her wisdom and inner resources. During the week she had spent with her, my sister had reduced our grandmother to near hysteria by disappearing from the house to wander around the barrio, causing talk among the neighbors. Abuelo had been recruited to keep track of Mili and to entertain her, but his efforts, too, had failed. Mili interrupted his endless lectures on literary and historical subjects with fantastical tales of her own in which movie actors were transformed into family members and family stories into movie scenarios, not always in comprehensible speech. Abuelo blamed Mili's behavior on the American television shows, which caused confusion in language for the impressionable young. At the end of the week Mili had spent without us, Abuela summoned my parents. Something had to be done about Mili. Our return trip across the island was silent and tense. When we arrived, we found my mother's sisters present too.

"Mamá Isadora once had a girl in her shop who had to be watched all the time or she would disappear," she said, beginning the session to which I had been invited, "but she had mastered the tiniest, most delicate stitch Mamá had ever seen. Her stitching was practically invisible, and all the customers asked that María Carmen de Dios sew for them. We all knew her as La Loca, poor *muchacha*. Putting a needle into María's hand was the only thing that calmed her down. Abuela said that it had been a trial for María's mother to get her to the shop every morning, since María Carmen de Dios was easily distracted by almost anything, and you know how boys are, they would whistle and call out her name. So the mother had to walk her by the hand to the *taller*. But once they sat her down and gave her a needle—it always had to be the right needle, since María Carmen de Dios knew exactly what kind of tool she needed for each detail of her work—then she would sew and sew all day. But any distraction, and off she went."

"Ay, Mamá, please don't tell stories like that. Mili is not crazy." Mami's voice was shaky and raw. As caught up as I was in my developing romance with Wilhelm, and my supposed birthday party, I had still been aware of her despair. Papi had been absent a lot lately too. And when he came home his gaze was distant. He read us the weekly letters from his brother, skipping, I could tell, over the parts about Patricio, and focusing on the news about good-paying jobs and incredible business opportunities. Tío Domingo was thinking about buying a small apartment building in New Jersey as a silent partner with a Jewish man named Peretz. Almost a Spanish name, Tío had pointed out. He wanted Papi to be the resident manager if it came through.

"He wants you to be the janitor," my mother had countered in a bitter tone. "You perform *that* service *and many others* right here at the Golden Palms. Why relocate to do the same thing?" Every word she spoke to him those days was charged with double meaning. She wanted him to know that she knew about the other women. Maybe it was also an appeal to him to quit before he forced her to do something drastic. I thought that maybe *he* had a counterplot going at the same time—that had worked for him once before. Since my mother believed that one way to get him away from an affair was to move us, he might agree to move but only if it were a move in a direction chosen by him. His internal compass seemed to be pointing north again. Given that we already lived at the northernmost point on the island, however, we would have to leave Puerto Rico or drown. I sensed that I was caught in a whirlpool that was sucking down my family. I began to understand Patricio's urgent need to escape from his father. But as a girl, without any contacts outside my relatives and my equally powerless school friends, I was adrift, lost at sea.

Tía Awilda, as the other mother of adolescent children, came to Mami's support. She said, "Nobody is saying that Mili is crazy, Angélica. Why, my own Miguelito has gone wild lately, playing his American records all day and all night in his room and acting like he is the center of the universe."

"He's a *machito*, hija. With men it's different. If he wasn't stretching his wings, getting ready to fly, you'd have something to worry about," Abuela said, then nodded in Mami's direction, "like the *tragedia* with the nephew." Abuela could never remember the names of my father's relatives beyond his deceased parents. All others lay outside her daughter's immediate *familia*, and thus outside Abuela's field of interest.

"What I'm saying, Mamá," my aunt continued, "is that many adolescents go through these stages. Angélica needs to get Mili back on track. It's not a serious thing, I'm sure."

Childless Tía Divina sided with Abuela. "I think Angélica should get help for Mili. Put her in a special school or take her to a psychiatrist." It was obvious from her self-assured tone that Tía Divina was enjoying being able to pass the mantle of *la mártir*, *la sufrida*, of always being the pitiful suffering sister, on to my mother. True, she didn't have children, her superior tone seemed to indicate, but at least she didn't have to deal with the shame of having a mentally ill daughter to explain to people.

But Mami was not going to accept the verdict of *loca* for her younger daughter quite so easily, and for once in her life she went beyond her mother and sisters for advice. When we brought Mili home from Abuela's, my mother made an unusual request of me. She made it clear that this was to be strictly between us; Papi could not know. She called me into the kitchen for a cup of coffee after school one day. Mili was still officially "sick" and staying home, since it had been decided that a solution to my sister's behavior problems had to be found before she could be sent back into a classroom.

Papi had dismissed Mili's problems at school by blaming them on the island's inferior school system and on Mili's former teacher, whom he called *La Mula*, the mule, because of her arrogant stubbornness. And because she was ugly too. He had no more to say about it. Having designated the problem as a *cosa de mujeres*, Papi had retreated to give us "women" room to solve it. We knew the only option he offered was moving us to the United States: "A new start away from all our old problems."

"Or a new place to take our old problems," Mami had countered, inciting yet another confrontation and another slamming of the front door—which left us home alone to deal with Mili. Mili herself seemed blithely unconcerned about the devastation she left in her wake as she retreated further into her own private world.

My fifteenth birthday was fast approaching, and still no mention of the party I had been promised.

"*Hija*"—Mami's fingers trembled as she placed the pink cup and saucer in front of me—"I need you to do something for me before your father gets home." She hid her weary face behind a thick puff of smoke; we both knew that Papi's hours had become highly unpredictable. He too was obviously troubled about Mili, who had always been his "doll," his future beauty queen or movie star. Sometimes I heard him come to my sister's bedroom door and sigh as if his heart were breaking. Some nights, sleepless in my bed, I listened to my mother's sobs in the kitchen while she waited for him to show up at any hour, then to his wanderings around the house. These sounds of lives falling apart during the night became as familiar to me as the sounds of our previous normal routines had once been. Night after night I waited for the inevitable unraveling of all the coiled pain in each of us.

My mother finally told me what she wanted. "Consuelo, I need you to go to Doña Sereno's house for me today."

"Why?" I had expected almost anything from my frantic

mother—a request to spy on Papi, to take care of Mili while she went somewhere, even a shoulder to cry on—but to go to María Sereno's mother's house, that came as a total surprise. The widow was practically a recluse. Nobody blamed her for that, since her son's oddness was enough reason to stay hidden from public sight. But Doña Sereno's visitors were usually "outside" people who came to consult with her as a spirit medium. It was not something that the matrons in our neighborhood admitted to doing themselves, even though Mami and her sisters often gossiped about others traveling across the island to see an *espiritista* in a town where nobody knew them.

Mami handed me a sealed envelope. "I'm asking her to give me a consultation about your sister." Mami's eyes were downcast as she said this, an attitude of humility she had not displayed before me until now. Her bowed head almost made me cry. I knew this was the last thing she could think to do before admitting that my sister was ill, ill beyond Mamá Isadora's wisdom, Abuela's home remedies, or anything she and Papi could buy at the new Walgreen's drugstore with its aisles of the latest American cures—cures for almost anything except my sister's mysterious illness.

I took the envelope that she had placed in the middle of the table. It was a windy day, indicating a surprise from the sea coming our way, a storm perhaps. I felt the soles of my feet burning through my sandals as I walked down the blinding white cement sidewalk in a straight line from our house to the end of our street, where Doña Sereno and her son lived. I tasted the sea salt in the air, and I remembered the taste of Wilhelm's kisses.

The room I found myself in, after the *¡Entre!* I barely heard, was thick with the smell of wax and incense. The other odors and aromas I could not identify, but there seemed to be layers of them, as if the blinds had not been opened in years. The place was so dimly lit that I had to wait a few seconds to adjust my vision from the blinding sun outside to the artificial dusk of Doña Sereno's living room. She sat at a table against the far wall. Behind her hung a crude oil painting of a woman in a flowing white gown carrying red roses. There was a wreath over the lady's temples, or what I thought was a wreath until my eyes adjusted fully. Then I saw that it was a crown of thorns, just like Christ wore to his crucifixion, with a similar pattern of blood droplets on her forehead. The bouquet of roses also had huge thorns and her fingers were bleeding. The odd thing about this picture was that the woman was smiling like a beauty queen taking her triumphant walk down the ramp. I must have been staring because Doña Sereno touched me with a waxy finger on my arm. I hadn't realized I had come so close to where she was sitting under the picture.

"In what way may I serve you, niña?" It was the usual question of a polite person to a stranger. I knew it meant she did not expect this to be a social call. I handed her the envelope from my mother. Doña Sereno's face did not express any emotion as she read my mother's message, but she looked directly into my eyes after she had put the note in her bosom. She was an almost pretty woman with a long nose and high cheekbones, but too thin. I saw the resemblance to María Sereno in her thick hair, which was cut shorter than his. Hers had streaks of silver in it. She looked like any of the other women in our barrio in her gray housedress suitable for a longtime widow, the *medio luto* that the generation before my mother's chose to wear in memory of their husbands, usually for life. Doña Sereno looked like a fully female version of her son, not frightening like I had expected her to be up close, except for her eyes, which fastened on mine like beams of light.

"Tell your mother to come when she's ready, with the girl. I'm always here."

"*Sí, señora.*" I took one last and, I hoped, discreet look around me, and walked out of Doña Sereno's house, nearly stumbling on a step in the sudden final brilliance of the setting sun.

Walking home that day, I felt eyes following me, though I saw no one on the porches. I knew some of our nosy neighbors were watching me through their blinds, so that later in their kitchens they could compare notes about the strange goings-on at my house. Mili spent all her time indoors now with my frantic mother looking in on her constantly or telling me to "keep an eye on your sister." Not that Mili was killing animals or doing anything more extraordinary than turning her gaze inward and moving her lips silently as if she had company inside her head. Other times, she chatted away about her usual interests, television shows and movies, never asking why she wasn't in school and practically a prisoner in our house. And now I was involved in some kind of secret conspiracy with my mother, to get my sister in the hands of a weird *espiritista* in case her problem was not of this world.

The day my mother chose to visit Doña Sereno with Mili was also my fifteenth birthday. There had been no mention of my supposedly special day at breakfast. Papi had casually announced that he'd be working late that night; in fact, he might not be home until the next morning. Mami had thrown her unbreakable cup into the sink from where she sat at the table, startling me out of my chair. The cup had careened over the counter, breaking a glass ashtray. No one spoke a word.

"*Bueno,*" Mami had finally said; it was a dismissal. There would be no arguments with Papi that day. She wanted him out of the house, even if it meant that he was at the Golden Palms with that *puta*, as she now referred to the singing maid even in front of her sisters, who pretended to be scandalized by Mami's new vulgar vocabulary. My mother didn't seem to care about "good" words or "bad" words so much these days.

Papi had turned bright red. He looked at Mami as if he wanted to say something, then he looked at me. He left the kitchen and soon I heard the car's engine and the screeching of the tires as he sped away.

For a long time I just sat at the table looking out the window toward the encroaching forest that had once been Patricio's backyard. The house had been sold to an American sailor whose family had not yet arrived. He used it like a hotel or camping area on weekends. The banana tree was burdened with fruit that ripened and fell over the spot that had once been the Lizard Lounge, and the flowering plants that my aunt had planted were entangled with weeds.

Mami finally broke the silence. "Consuelo." She got her cup out of the sink and refilled it with black coffee, lighting up again. There were three Salem butts in the Golden Palms ashtray. "Hija, I am taking Mili over to Doña Serena's this afternoon, if she'll see me. Do you want to come with us?"

For a brief moment I had entertained the hope that Mami had at least remembered the day she had given birth to me. "Can't I just go to the English club meeting and out for a hamburger with Marisa after school?" I had a cry in my throat but swallowed it down. I was planning to celebrate my birthday anyway, even if no one in my family did. No tears for me today. It was my day.

Mami nodded absently, blowing smoke out through her nose, a sight that repelled me. I heard Mili humming a popular merengue as I passed her room. It was all the same to her to stay home in her baby-doll pajamas watching the variety shows with Mami. Her life was not lived in the same time frame as ours anyway. I wished peace for her, that she could choose her life, but already her "vacation" was coming to an end. The school board had given my parents an ultimatum: Mili would have to be dragged back out to face reality. It seemed to me that she was better off where she was.

I discussed my plans to meet Wilhelm that night with Marisa in school, though not all the details, in case I didn't have the courage to do it. She agreed to cover for me if she had to. I wasn't really concerned about getting caught in a lie by my parents. They were too busy with their problems to care about what I did. Marisa couldn't believe they had forgotten my birthday. She said she had a gift for me she'd give me later. "Not everyone forgot your birthday." She winked at me, acting as if she knew something I didn't.

After the English club meeting, Wilhelm was waiting as usual outside the gymnasium. We had been spending a lot of time together lately. He had just showered and he smelled of cologne and soap. I asked him to go with me to the new hamburger joint. A New York–born *puertorriqueña*, a *Nuyorican* as she called herself, had just opened La Cafetería Josefina, now called Josey's Burger. We sat at a table in the back and ordered in English. Josey shouted our order to the cook in her Brooklyn accent.

"*Oye*, whatsamarawiya, ha? I tolya, *sabes, que* hurry up *con esa orden!*" She yelled at her cook constantly. He worked at a Puerto Rican snail's pace while she whirled through the place like she was fighting traffic in New York, offending everyone equally with her colorful language and occasional obscene gesture. But she was good at business, and if you looked beyond her tough Nuyorican façade, maybe she was a good person too.

Wilhelm liked this place because his Spanish seemed impeccable compared to Josey's.

He put a little box on the table between us while I listened to Josey threatening the cook once again.

"Open it." Wilhelm pushed it toward me since I was just staring at it.

It was a pinky ring with a tiny purple amethyst, my birthstone. I put it on my little finger with some difficulty since I was trembling.

"It's called a friendship ring," he said, taking my fingers in his big hands.

"*Gracias,*" I mumbled, taken down a notch by the word *friendship.* I didn't expect it to be an engagement ring, but I didn't think of Wilhelm as merely my friend. He was my obsession.

"You like it?"

I nodded and he leaned over and kissed me lightly on the lips.

"Hey, hey! No smooching in my establishment, you two," Josey yelled from the kitchen. "I don't want her papi coming here and shooting everybody! *¿Entienden?*" Josey had the idea that all Puerto Rican men were jealous and violent, and all the women on the island sissies who put up with them. She expressed these views freely to the high-school kids who frequented her restaurant. Her burger joint was thriving anyway. Josey's disdain for the "natives" was returned in equal measure by our parents, who made fun of the way she couldn't say three words in Spanish without falling into her Spanglish, but it didn't bother us.

Wilhelm and I ate slowly so that by the time we started our walk toward my house it was getting dark.

"Will you get in trouble?"

"Nobody's home."

As the bright lights of the city gave way to the less well illuminated streets of my neighborhood, I moved closer to Wilhelm. He was a head taller than I, so he leaned his whole body toward me. We had to slow our pace in order to synchronize our steps. I felt his heat and smelled his salty aroma. When we got to my block, he abruptly let go of my hand. He knew he had to be cautious about vigilant island parents. But I held on to his elbow.

"Let's keep walking."

When we passed my house, I saw that the kitchen light was on, as was the television. I could tell from the flickering lights, reflected on the blinds. Mami and Mili were home. I pulled the reluctant Wilhelm down the street. He laughed, allowing me to hurry him toward the dark end of the block.

"Where are you taking me, niña?"

"You'll see. And don't call me a niña anymore, okay?"

"Okay, señorita. Just don't pull my arm off. I'll go in peace."

I lightly touched his lips with my fingers. *"Silencio,"* I whispered, leading him toward the back of María Sereno's house and into the secret place I had chosen—a sort of grotto made by the fallen leaves of palm trees that would soon be cut down by a construction crew. For now the little bower of warm sandy earth and sweet-smelling banana plant leaves was a sanctuary like the ones Patricio and I had created in his backyard.

The only light came dimly through the window of María Sereno's bedroom. It was enough to show me the way into the cave of trees and plants leaning their branches one over the other in a sort of embrace. Wilhelm had to bend almost double to follow me in.

"Do you know where you're going?" he whispered, as I pulled him down into a bed of leaves softened by dew.

"Sí." I covered his mouth with mine, hoping that he knew more than I did about what I wanted to happen next.

I emerged from the trees with Wilhelm by my side. He seemed to have nothing to say. What had happened in the dark had not transformed me into a woman as I had hoped. It had been more like a painful wrestling match. And now, with dry leaves tangled in my mossy hair, scratched from rocks on my back, I felt more like a child who'd gotten her Sunday clothes dirty. We walked in silence to the edge of my yard, where I pulled his face down and kissed his cheek. He smelled of the leaves we had lain on and of sweat, and of a wild sweet smell new to me. He plucked a dry petal from my hair and I took it from his hand and kissed his fingers one by one. I said good night. He did not answer, merely nodded, his eyes distant. Then he turned and walked away.

It wasn't supposed to be like this. I wanted some kind words, a last kiss, some acknowledgment that this had meant something to him. But he had not even looked back. I watched his tall lanky form disappear into the shadows beyond the sparse lampposts of my street, and I wondered whether he too felt the confusion I was experiencing. But I checked any further thoughts at the door to my house, fearing that my mother would read my mind as she had often done in the past when I had tried to hide something from her. Later, alone in my bed, I could recall the experience; bring it to life in my head, read it like a forbidden book.

I was thankful that for once Mami was not waiting for me as I came into our dark living room. My parents were in the kitchen talking in low, tense voices. Although I wondered why Papi had come home early, I didn't really want to know. I passed Mili's room on tiptoe, hoping that I could just say a quick good night to my parents without being summoned into the brightly lit kitchen where they might see my wrinkled clothes, stained with dirt and crushed leaves. But it was my sister who called out my name softly. She was in her bed with the covers drawn up to her chin. Her face was wet with tears, and when I sat down next to her she pulled my head down.

"Consuelito, I'm scared," she said in a voice she had not been using much lately. It was her own normal voice speaking in our shared language, not the secret code she used when she turned inward and away from us.

"What are you afraid of, Mili?"

"I don't know. Sometimes, Consuelito, I think I hear my body growing in the dark. I am stretching too tight because my skin doesn't fit, and then what? I don't want to break into pieces."

"It will be all right, Mili. You were just dreaming."

"I only dream when I am awake, Consuelo. *La noche, la noche* is too long for me to dream a dream. It would kill me to have a dream that lasted all night long."

"Just close your eyes, Mili. I will stay here with you while you sleep. You don't have to dream."

As I tried to comfort her I remembered a day when we had been driving across the island toward Abuela's house. We had stopped outside the coastal town of Ponce to eat at Papi's favorite seafood restaurant. It had a terrace over the water and a long pier. While we waited for the food, Mili and I walked down the pier to the gazebo where the lights attracted schools of shrimp. They thought it was the moon, I had heard, and that's how fishermen caught them. The sky suddenly turned a deep purple at the horizon, and we saw a funnel cloud begin to form from the patch of color, shaping itself as if an invisible potter was at the wheel. The funnel dropped a thin curling tail into the water and began to snake toward land. The sight had transfixed Mili; her face took on a look of religious ecstasy. Then she started chanting a mantra in a made-up language. I recognized the rhythms; it was like the Kyrie we said in church during mass.

"*Aguazul, aguacero, aguabuena, aguamala, aguardiente, marysol, marycielo,* Consuelo, Consuelo."

I had listened carefully, trying to make sense of her words, all connected by sound. It seemed there was some kind of poetry at its core. I thought that maybe she was calling my name, maybe trying to help me see what she saw. But I had also been aware that the people who rushed to the balcony for a view of the waterspout were now staring and pointing at Mili. Maybe they thought what the crazy girl said was nonsense. But I believed that something had made my sister almost unbearably happy. Maybe it was the brilliant blue of the ocean that day. Whatever it was I wanted to understand it and share her happiness. But Papi had hurried down to escort us back to our table, his face red with shame. In the meantime, Mami had canceled our dinner order. I saw her looking, with anger or fear in her eyes, at the waterspout now grown to half the size of the horizon. "It's coming this way," she finally said, as if to herself, and taking Mili by the hand, she had rushed to the car ahead of my father and me.

I stroked Mili's hair and held her like Mami used to hold us, close and tight against my body, now bruised and swollen from Wilhelm's violent caresses, and I rocked her like a baby. I understood the wild beating of her heart, and I felt her fear pass through her hot skin into mine like a fever. Maybe on that night Mili and I were afraid of the same thing—that we were never going to be like the others around us.

AGUACERO: Heavy Rain; a Downpour

We had become a family who lived a secret life after dark. After my sister fell asleep on the night of the day I turned fifteen and I had retreated to my own room, my mother came in and sat down on my bed.

"Consuelo, I need to speak with you right now, hija. Are you awake?"

"I am now." I hoped my brusque tone let her know that I wanted her out of my room. She had not remembered the day when she had brought me into the world, but if I were to tell her how I had celebrated it, she would never forget again. By the sliver of light she had let in through the door I could see that she was dressed in a black cocktail dress and high heels. I moved away from her, turning my face to the wall.

"Hija, I know how you feel. We will make this day up to you soon. But there are problems in this family that I have to deal with now, before they become . . ."

"A *tragedia*," I interrupted her sarcastically.

"Let us hope you understand when you become . . ."

"A *mujer*," I finished for her. Her vocabulary list for our family emergencies was well known to me. But my insolence caught her by surprise.

"Enough, Consuelo!" She got up from my bed. "Listen to me. Your father and I have to go out tonight. You should know that it's a grave matter and that you have to do your part."

"Where are you going?"

"To the Golden Palms."

There was a brief silence. I think she was waiting for me to ask her why she was going to Papi's workplace on a weeknight at this hour. But I didn't.

"I'll watch Mili." I was curt. I would do my duty as always—the serious, sane, and dependable daughter.

"I need you to sleep in her room tonight, Consuelo. We had a visit from her teacher today—it was hard on Mili."

"What happened at Doña Sereno's house?" I had a feeling that the visit to the medium's house had been what really upset my sister.

"That's another matter. We'll talk more tomorrow. Your father is waiting for me."

I heard the Studebaker revving up as Mami walked out the front door. I gathered my blankets and pillow. Mili was sleeping fitfully on the edge of her narrow princess bed. I made myself a nest on the cool tile floor in her room. Finally, after the car pulled away, the house fell into a heavy silence, like that before a tropical thunderstorm.

I thought about what I had done with Wilhelm just a few hours ago, trying to place it in the context of what I knew about sex: not much beyond the clinical facts which I had gotten out of the *Britannica*, women's gossip, and the stories in Abuelo's old books about the free and easy mating customs of the Indians before the Spanish "civilized" them. The talk at my school was always about the girls who "did it," but I had never gotten their stories firsthand since none of my friends had done it. Or if they had, I didn't know about it. Now I had done it. And it couldn't be undone.

I remembered Wilhelm's rough hands pulling my clothes away from my body, as if I were a package wrapped in layers; the smell of the moist earth I could almost taste as his weight pressed down on me; and his fierceness, as if he were my opponent in a wrestling match. I wanted to ask him to slow down, to be gentler: I wanted to savor this experience, and besides it hurt. But it was as if he had forgotten I was there.

When it was over, Wilhelm got dressed without a word. I could barely see him in the dark, but I heard the clinking of his belt buckle and his labored breathing. Still he didn't say anything. Adjusting my eyes to the darkness, I detected that he was staring at the house next door where a loud radio had started playing the latest mambo hit. Slivers of light came into our hiding place as the window blinds were opened wider. I suddenly felt exposed. Wilhelm continued to watch the house as I buttoned my blouse and smoothed my skirt down. I knew he was afraid of getting caught out there with me. There would be no explaining it. I wiped myself with my underwear and stuffed it in my skirt pocket. We crawled out of our secret place like escaped convicts, and walked apart in silence toward my house.

The romantic movies that Mili and I saw showed couples lingering over each other's lips, moving slowly around each other's bodies as in a bolero, heading inexorably toward the act that would not be shown on screen. I had thought that sex would be like a slow dance, that making love was a melding of flesh and soul, not merely a clash of bones and meat. I was not a total fool. I had not expected passionate words of love from Wilhelm, but neither had I anticipated the almost hostile silence. Why was Wilhelm angry with me when I had given him the only thing a girl had to give that was hers alone? All else, including my past and my future, belonged to my parents, at least for many years to come.

"I'm afraid," I said to myself, curling up on the cold hard floor in Mili's room.

It was very late, almost daybreak, when the front door opened, nearly time for the alarm to go off in my room. I did not hear my parents speak, only their shuffling noises as they moved around rooms, checking the house. I heard the shower and my father's usual sounds of dressing for work. But no words. It was as if my family's clock had been reversed. We communicated at night in urgent whispers; during daylight hours we walked around doing what other people did, pretending we were normal.

The morning after Mami went with Papi to the Golden Palms, I found her at her usual post in the kitchen. She had a cup of black coffee in one hand, a cigarette with half an inch of ash in the other, and was still wearing the black sequined dress and patent-leather high heels. She had obviously not been to bed. I'd had only a couple of hours of sleep myself. As if I had placed an order at a bar, she poured me a cup of coffee and slid it in front of me. I felt like an impostor in my crisp white blouse, which she had ironed, and my pleated uniform skirt. Could anybody tell that I wasn't a señorita anymore? Could she see any difference on my face? I had studied myself in the mirror that morning. I was skinny, but my breasts were fuller, my body rounder. There were also dark purplish rings under my eyes that made me look older. It had been weeks since I had slept a whole night through, and my headaches had returned full force. But I no longer told anyone about them. Pain was mine too. I could own it.

"You look sick, niña. Did Mili keep you awake last night? She was so worked up yesterday, I was afraid she'd walk out of the house. That's why I asked you to sleep in her room."

"She slept all night, Mami." I was weary. Suddenly the roles were reversed and my mother was tiptoeing around whatever she really wanted to say to me, being overly solicitous—a tactic she employed when she wanted to ask me to do something difficult. "When is she going back to school?"

"Mili can't go back to her old school, Consuelo. That's one of the things I need to tell you. The school nurse showed up here with a psychologist the school board hired. I don't know how they did it, but after spending less than an hour locked up with your sister in her room, they came out and informed me that *they* had decided she needs professional care." My mother sighed, scrunching her eyes shut for a minute as if she wanted tears to come out, but the well was dry.

"Did they say what's wrong with her?"

"They didn't give it a name, hija. They say we need to have her evaluated by a psychiatrist before she will be allowed in a classroom again."

She fell silent, biting the tip of her thumb in an almost childish way. I waited for her to get to the point. My role in this would soon be made clear.

"It was a hard day, yesterday. Your birthday, *mi amor*. Don't think I forgot. I'll make it up to you . . ."

"Forget it."

"Someday you'll understand, Consuelo. We are going through a test from God. This family, *I* am being tested. It's my—"

"Cross to bear." I finished the sentence for her. But this time she just smiled bitterly, not bothering to call me on my affront. When she spoke again she was more like herself. Crushing the cigarette fiercely in the Golden Palms ashtray, she sipped her coffee slowly, staring me down across the table. Once I had lowered my eyes, she said, "I met the woman last night. She's a pile of bones wrapped in bright rags. A *trapo*, the kind you use to wipe up dog piss from the floor. Your father has been blinded by her empty promises of recording that old song of his."

"He took you to meet her?"

"It was either that or I was going by myself."

"So what happened?"

"Nothing much. Except I told him to choose. Either come home with me and never see *esa mujer* again, or stay with her and never come home again."

"What would you have done if he'd chosen her?"

"Packed you and Mili up and gone to my mother's casa. There is something you should understand, hija: family is all a woman can really count on. A woman's loyalty is to her husband, but when he betrays her, the children belong to her. If she's lucky, she can always go to her mother's house. Women can count on each other."

"If I did something wrong, would you always take me back?"

"If you are *decente* I will always be here for you, Consuelo. That is one of the few rewards in a good woman's life."

"What about Mili? What did Doña Sereno tell you to do about her?"

"I'm coming to that. This all revolves around your sister. *¿Entiendes?* If it wasn't that I am desperate to find help for her, I would just tell him to go to hell with his tramp." She paused for a moment, squeezing her eyes shut as if to fight tears. "Doña Sereno advised me to confront the *malas influencias* trying to destroy this family. Your father's *aventuras* are at the core of all our troubles."

She lit another cigarette, inhaling deeply, as if it were the oxygen she needed to go on living. When she finally exhaled, slowly releasing a cloud between us, she seemed calmer. "We are going to New York, Consuelo. Papi says he can find Mili good doctors and a special school there."

I held my breath. My whole body tensed, ready for battle. I inhaled so that my voice would sound calm. "I don't want to go."

"It has nothing to do with what we want now, hija. We are going to do what we *have* to do. Either that, or we can each pack our bags and head out in different directions. Besides, the hotel is being sold. He expects to be laid off soon."

"Why don't we just go back to your mother's?"

"That is not a choice anymore. She will not accept us in her home if there is any chance of my marriage working out."

"No matter what price we have to pay."

It was not a question and she did not try to answer me. Instead, she gave me a sealed envelope; again, I was to be the messenger in the *tragedia* of the fall of the house of Signe. The envelope was for La Señora. I was to hand-deliver it to Mili's teacher after school. Our fate was sealed inside this letter, too.

Doña Sereno had advised my mother to confront the *malas influencias* entering our home. She was to look evil in the face and challenge it in the name of the Holy Mother. Had not the Holy Mother held her grown son in her arms after his own friend had betrayed him? It was a woman's silent defiance that had shown an idolatrous world that a woman's love for her child is more powerful than the laws of men or their ridicule. My mother would do whatever it took to save this *familia*. She would put on her golden armor of martyrdom and become La Sufrida.

I did not see Wilhelm until the end of the day at basketball practice. I walked through the gym. In the past, he had always managed to call time-out so we could talk, or to find some other way of acknowledging me. But he seemed impervious to me that afternoon, even though I walked very slowly toward the girls' locker room, the only area I was allowed in, and then slowly back across the expanse

of polished wood that now seemed as large as a continent and as revealing as a mirror under my feet. I glanced back once and caught
him looking in my direction with a strange grin on his face. Papito
Morales and a couple of the other players were also staring at me
with similar amused expressions. I felt the pressure at the crown of
my skull that warned me of a coming explosion of pain. Hurrying
out, I almost crashed into my homeroom teacher, Miss Vélez, who
had apparently been waiting for me at the entrance to the gym.

I tried to avoid her, but she called me over. I felt it was only a
matter of minutes before my blinding headache struck. The familiar throbbing was starting.

"I have to get this to my sister's teacher." I showed her the
letter.

"She's my neighbor. I can make sure she gets it." She grabbed
the envelope and my elbow, leading me down the covered breeze-
way toward her classroom. I breathed the humid air; rain was coming, a downpour. Usually the rainy season was something I looked
forward to; I liked getting drenched in the afternoon showers that
often started at precisely the hour we were let out of school. Right
before an *aguacero*, Mili and I would put our books in plastic trash
bags, then we'd take our time going home, strolling while others
ran as the rain came down harder, letting the warm water fill our
shoes so they squished with every step. We laughed like little kids
as we got completely drenched. Mami was unusually lenient about
our rain-induced craziness. I suspected she herself had danced in
the rain once or twice in her life. The only rule was that we head
for the shower without any detours. But I doubted that this year
there would be any singing or dancing in the rain for any of us.

Miss Vélez led me to a chair next to her book-laden desk.

"Consuelo, I suppose your mother has told you about your
sister's problem?"

I nodded, concentrating on reading the titles of the books

stacked precariously on the desk: *Diccionario*/Dictionary, *La Música Folklórica de Puerto Rico, Puerto Rico: Free Associated Commonwealth: What Does It Mean?* And a thin book, almost too thin to read the title on the spine, but I recognized it: *Songs of the Simple Truth*, the poems of Julia de Burgos.

"You don't look well, niña. Perhaps you should go to the clinic. I can have the school nurse . . ."

"Please, no señora." My words came out more abruptly than I intended, but the pressure at my temples was increasing.

"It's señorita, not señora, thank you." She removed the thick glasses from her long Spanish nose and fixed me with her green eyes. She looked like a *gringa* with that pale skin, brown hair turning gray at the temples, and snake eyes. "And it's 'Miss' by choice, whatever you might think. Señorita."

Her sarcasm was too much for me to take along with my exploding head. I jumped out of the chair, hoping to escape before the tears came. But she had anticipated me. Standing directly in front of me, she placed one hand on my shoulder. I thought she was going to hit me or drag me to the principal's office. But instead, she raised my chin with one long finger so I was looking her in the eyes. The usual sternness was gone. She was looking at me with concern. What did she know? Was this about my family's problems, or about Wilhelm and me?

"Consuelo, it's up to you to save yourself, hija." Perhaps she would have explained what she meant by those words if I had not run out, just in time to get around the corner and vomit into some hibiscus bushes. I sank to my knees in agony. There was a roll of thunder in the distance and soon the sky turned black and let go like a dam breaking. The water was a blessing on my head. By the time I got home, my headache had eased to a dull throb and my empty stomach made me feel purified, like I did after one of Abuela's herbal remedies.

SEÑORITA

When I got home, there was a letter from Patty Swan along with a couple of other pieces of wet mail lying on my pillow. Mami had apparently rescued them from our leaky mailbox as the rain started.

Dear Consuelo,

I am finally settled in a new apartment, or should I say closet? It is so small that I have to step out onto the fire escape to change my mind. But good news! I am making money doing what I like to do: drawing and painting. I have become the "apprentice" (one of many) of a famous interior designer here in New York. I showed him some sketches (you remember the ones I did of buildings in Old San Juan) I *happened* to bring with me to a party where I *happened* to know I'd run into him, and he was immediately impressed!

I remain cash poor, but I am free. I hear my father is still making trouble for me by asking people to turn me in to the police if they see me. But I have friends too. He'll never find me in this city. Did you know that his partner backed out on their deal and now he's saddled with an apartment building in New Jersey that white people won't move into? He was stupid to think that he could be a landlord in an Italian neighborhood. He's now "recruiting" tenants to move to New Jersey from the Hispano community here. He put an ad in *La Prensa*: only *gente decente* need apply. I may try to rent an apartment from him. You think I qualify (joke)?

Well, *mi amor*, you can write to Patty Swan at this address until she starts making enough money to move to a bigger place. How is your romance with our boy Wilhelm going? And your *quinceañera*? I bet it was the social event of the season in San Juan. I want to know all the details!

Con amor,
Patty

Patricio's letter infuriated me. It was all about *him*. His questions about Wilhelm and my birthday were a joke, an afterthought. It was obvious he didn't care about my pain now that he had another life far from my little daily *tragedias*.

I fell into a heavy sleep only to be startled awake by the sound of knocking on my bedroom door.

"Yes?"

My mother came in with something wrapped in a torn page of newsprint. She showed me my bloody underwear. I sat up, my heart beating wildly. She knew!

"Consuelo. I found these in the hamper today. Can you please remember to take care of your own things during that time of the month? Your father could have seen them."

"I'm sorry," I mumbled, almost bursting into tears from relief.

"It's just not proper for men to see these things. I thought I told you that when you became a señorita."

"You did, Mami. It won't happen again."

"I'll leave them here for you to wash by hand. Better get used to doing this, as unpleasant as it is. When you get married it will be worse, you'll have to handle your husband's dirty things too." She made herself shiver in disgust.

"At least they don't bleed." I made my voice sound even, though I was trembling.

"No, but they make other messes."

Then she went out to hang clothes in the backyard, leaving me with that little mystery to ponder.

Mili was kept home most of the year, visited by counselors sent from school. Soon after her eleventh birthday, she started menstruating. Luckily, I heard her cries of distress first since, at the sight of blood on her white shorts, she had removed all her clothes. She seemed paralyzed by the sight of her own blood. She pointed at the soiled clothing, making the same hiccuping noises of distress that she had made as a toddler. I handed her a robe and cleared a space on her bed for us to sit. Her room was, as usual, covered with fan magazines and photos of celebrities that she had begun to cut out for her album. According to her test scores, she was still above average in her reading and math skills, though her ability to communicate verbally was deteriorating. The school board had officially advised my parents they had the rest of the academic year to determine a course of action for Mili, to find either an institution or a special school. Papi had turned in his resignation at work. And Mami had begun giving away everything that we would not be able to pack in a few boxes.

Things were happening too fast for me too. I wondered whether Mili sensed the tension around her and was reverting to the safety of her imaginary world, where she could continue being taken care of like an infant. That day I comforted my sister as best I could, then sent Mami in with the blue box of sanitary napkins.

Abuela called the family together again to discuss Mili's deteriorating condition. The women were worried. Now that Mili was a señorita, there would be different problems to consider: she was so childlike in her trust of people and enticed by the novelty of strangers that men could easily take advantage of her. My mother brought up my name only to praise my attention to my sister, my serious and studious nature. Unlike most fifteen-year-olds, especially in this new world of teenage rebellion, I stayed home a lot, studying English, reading novels and poetry, and spending time with Mili. In fact, Mami said, I understood Mili's strange vocabulary better than anyone. She took great comfort in her good daughter. Tía Awilda added that she was glad I wasn't boy crazy, and Tía Divina chimed in that even her youngest, Rafaelito, was showing an interest in the opposite sex, but that was *normal* for pubescent boys. Girls could take longer to mature sexually.

"If girls only knew what it was we have to put up with to have children," Abuela shook her head in disgust, "they wouldn't be in such a hurry."

This was the signal for each of the women to tell her tale of heartbreak and pain, so I stopped listening and went outside. Lying in the hammock on the porch, I rocked myself gently. I remembered how sweet it had been at first with Wilhelm and me, and how suddenly everything had changed between us.

Wilhelm had betrayed me. He and Marisa were *novios* now, a couple at school, but in secret, since her parents did not approve of his family. Marisa and I were not speaking. I heard that she had been *shocked* by what I had done. In fact, everything had been turned upside down. I had lost Wilhelm by giving myself to him. I no longer had Marisa as a friend, and she had Wilhelm.

My father would be unemployed as of May when he resigned from the Golden Palms Hotel. And we would be in a different country in a matter of months. I found that I cared less each day about leaving. I had begun to understand why my father did not take pleasure in the fact that one could see the ocean from almost any high spot on the island. There was no place to hide here. We were all exposed to the punishing sun.

My cousin Miguel, an arrogant seventeen-year-old that year, sat in the hammock, almost causing me to fall off. He was already tall and built like an athlete, a baseball player with potential, some believed. Traveling all over the island with the Police Athletic League team, he barely made it from grade to grade at school. But he was considered *guapo*, attractive to women of all ages. The girls at my school had even deigned to speak to me on the day his team played ours, in hope of meeting him. I didn't go to the game. Everyone spoke of Miguel as if he were the catch of the century. And he knew it. Though the boy cousins had been separated from us as soon as we had begun to enter puberty, Miguel had never re-ally been interested in Mili or me. He was his mamá's little prince. She waited on him and spoiled him. I had begun to dislike him years before, and I believed it was reciprocal. So it surprised me when he slipped one of his big hands under the back of my shirt, discreetly, so that if one of the women happened to walk out she'd think we were just talking together like good friends. But his touch was not brotherly. I tried to squirm away. He leaned his muscular body over my legs, holding me down on Abuela's woven hammock where we had both been rocked to sleep as babies.

"What the hell do you think you're doing, Miguel?"

"I'm just trying to be friends with my favorite *prima*, Consuelito. I know you need a friend." Miguel's smile was wolfish: long white teeth and the full lips that were a dominant trait in Mami's family. I felt his fingers move down my spine as if he were playing piano. I stopped struggling.

"Let's go for a bicycle ride, *prima*. I want to take you to a place you haven't been before. Or maybe you have. But not with me." He grinned and nodded in the direction of the parlor. My move.

Although I knew my mother didn't think it was proper for me to go off alone with my cousin, I had earned her trust through months of self-sacrifice. Tía Awilda raised an eyebrow at her son when we came in to tell them that we would like to go for a bicycle ride. He blew her a kiss as we left. It was a strange sense of power I felt as I left the women sitting in their circle, thinking that their morality lessons had turned their daughters into armored virgins. I was angry at them for their blindness, angry at Wilhelm for turning out to be just like the villains in the women's cuentos; most of all, though, I wanted to test myself, to see who I really was.

I pedaled slowly behind my cousin, who led me out of the pueblo toward the open countryside, where sun-drowsy cows watched us pass by, chewing their cud like old ladies who would start gossiping as soon as we were out of sight. The road took us past pastures and toward the beach. The humidity was high. I was drenched in sweat and panting when Miguel finally pulled up by the side of a footpath lined with palm trees and vines. We left our bikes chained to a tree where the road ended at the edge of a thick grove of palms, and we walked toward a little square of light. In the clearing there was an army tent pitched with the remains of a campfire and a few beer cans littering the sand around it.

"Welcome to my *casita*, dear cousin. Do you like it?"

"Isn't it illegal to camp on the public beach?"

"Not for me. I have friends in high places, niña. Would you like to step in and have a little refreshment with me?"

There was a rough army blanket covering the floor, and a bucket with bottles of Old Colony grape drink and India beer cans floating in it. A card table and folding chairs were pushed into a corner and there was a hurricane lamp sitting on top.

"Care for a game of dominoes?" Miguel laughed. "I'm afraid the ice melted, Consuelito. But the English drink beer at room temperature. Did you know that? And they are a very civilized people." His demeanor was exactly like that of the men the women were always complaining about. Brash, always bragging about the privileges they enjoyed as males, the beer they consumed during the all-night domino games, what they had said or done to women, how they, as machos, had defended their territory or claimed their rights that day, or were going to the next. But there was something that told me that Miguel was calling my bluff.

"I'll have the Old Colony."

"You disappoint me, *prima*. I thought I *heard* that you were more adventurous." But his hand shook as he handed me the bottle.

"Shut up, Miguel," I said, pulling him down on the scratchy blanket. I stood up and began to take off my T-shirt.

"Consuelo . . ." His voice had a distinct note of fear as I finished undressing. I stood there before him naked, trying not to break into tears. I was hoping I knew Miguel for the coward he was.

"Well, *primo*. Is this what you wanted?"

"Are you a *puta*, Consuelo?"

I slapped him as hard as I could and he fell backward. Slowly I put on my clothes. I felt no shame. Only one thought had passed through my mind when I had taken off my last piece of clothing and stood naked: I belong to myself. I was not like my mother who had to get the permission of all her relatives and ancestors before making any decisions about her life. She was ruled by ghosts and their dead words: *la decencia, el sacrificio, el deber de la mujer buena, para la familia*. But in the end, had these magic formulas saved any of us from pain? It was time to learn a new language.

"Define the word *puta*, Miguelito, and I'll tell you if I'm a whore."

He didn't say another word. At least my cousin had learned when to simply shut his mouth. Above us raindrops spattered on the taut green canvas tent, an afternoon shower. By the time we got home, it was raining hard, a real *aguacero* that pelted my back and my face with the force of tiny, sharp stones. Throwing back my head, I tasted salt on my lips and tongue.

Sticks, Stones, and BOMBAS

María Sereno had injected cooking oil in his chest so he could have breasts. His jiggly walk toward the snow-cone man every day became a daily spectacle in our neighborhood. The people came out on their porches for his parade of one, making loud comments about the size, weight, and movement of his globes. He displayed them in a halter top he had fashioned out of a T-shirt emblazoned with the symbol and motto of Governor Muñoz Marín's party: the silhouette of a *jívaro* wearing a straw *pava*, and the words ¡JALDA ARRIBA! UPHILL ALL THE WAY. The message was clear: the journey of our island into the future had begun, and the common people would be leading the way. María Sereno had cut his T-shirt into a plunging V-neck halter. His cleavage was impressive, but even from a distance the mounds pushed up for display looked more like water-filled balloons than flesh.

Some weekend afternoons I sat in my mother's green metal rocker, an innovation over the wood-and-straw *sillones* small-town people still had in their homes (there was always something better,

Papi said; in other countries there was always someone working on an improved model of everything), and I watched María Sereno walk down the middle of a line of verbal fire. He smiled his enigmatic smile and sometimes tossed his head this way and that, letting the people know that he heard them, I supposed. The one-legged *piragüero* had started a sort of competition for *bombas* and *plenas*, off-color verses singsonged to the accompaniment of clapping or drumming on any available surface. This kind of vulgar musical play, Abuela had told me, had always been around in Puerto Rico. It was a sort of insult/duel set to the rhythms of two drums called bombas and *maracas*; a bawdy form of courtship, she said, begun by the African slaves in the *haciendas* to mock authority, and then adopted by the *campesinos*. It had to do with offers in crude rhymes made by the men, usually double-entendre sexual offers that were answered by a woman backed up by a chorus of her friends.

María Sereno is celebrating today.
How do I know?
By the bombas on her chest.
I would like to have them on board myself.

The *piragüero* began reciting as soon as he saw María Sereno coming down the sidewalk toward his pushcart, putting into play the other meanings of the word *bomba*—balloon or bomb—to the amusement of some of our neighbors who had taken front-row seats on their porches. I myself was curious as to what everyone's reaction to this spectacle would be.

Then, Doña Fifí, a seventy-year-old woman who still led the hymns at church with her powerful alto, sang her latest plena to the ever-growing song by projecting her voice from her porch rocker:

Oye, oye, macho with no shame,
Better release your serpent
In any woman's garden
Than in your neighbor's dark cave.

Yet María Sereno seemed to get bolder the more he was mocked. In fact, he sang a verse I had thought was meant for me as he passed by, not looking at me, but leaning his body in a ridiculous way, like a listing ship, toward my house.

Niña, niña, how deep is your well?
I heard him digging for fresh water
In your yard last night.
Did your river swell?

The show went on for several weeks, until the day María Sereno collapsed in front of his mother's house, bursting one of his "balloons" on the hot cement. The ambulance came and everyone watched Doña Sereno holding her unconscious son's hand as he was laid on a stretcher and taken away.

In the days that followed, no one offered to take Doña Sereno to the hospital to see her son. For weeks afterward, I watched her take slow careful steps—rheumatoid arthritis, I had heard, one of the many reasons she didn't leave her house much—as she walked the half mile to the nearest bus stop. She looked straight ahead, passing our car parked in the driveway, our neighbors' cars parked in theirs. I noticed that she held her head at a cocky angle just like her son, as if there were a crown on top of it instead of that mound of glossy hair. She held her chin up and slightly tilted, like a high-wire artist, as if nothing really mattered except taking one step and then the next without falling.

I felt my own head lift involuntarily, unconsciously imitating her, someone who would not allow herself to be defeated by words, even if they were thrown like stones by the same people who so often sought her help—but always in secret, because they were ashamed of being seen talking with the mother of a freak. She told them the truth, and they hated her for it. But they always came back to her in their darkest hour.

Maybe it was because it was to be my last spring on the island, but I noticed everything around me in an intense new way. Colors seemed so bright they hurt my eyes, the air tasted saltier, and the heat more intense. Due to the abundant rains that season, our neighbors' yards had exploded in overgrown grass, flowers, and ripe fruit. The tiny yellow-and-black warblers called *reinitas* were attracted to the sweet smells of the cassia and breadfruit trees, and I could step outside our sanitized air-conditioned house and experience a riot of earth smells right in my barrio. Mili sat in her swing for hours in the mild afternoons while I read the novels and books of poems that had taken the place of the encyclopedia volumes I had completely devoured in the past year and a half. Reaching the letter Z had been a letdown. I didn't feel any wiser, merely full of mostly useless facts that so far were irrelevant to my life—all in alphabetical order.

School was a penance I was doing for a few more weeks. Leading a double life of the good daughter at home and the "untouchable" among my "respectable" friends at school had worn me out. Not that I couldn't have all the company I wanted. There were groups of kids bused in from the fringes of San Juan who led wild lives that we heard about in our homes as *escándalos*.

I never ran into those girls at the places we frequented, never thought about them after my problems with Wilhelm. My mistake had been, I was informed by one of *those* girls, that I should have chosen more carefully. That is what Lucila Nieves, who was quitting school at the end of the school year to marry a thirty-year-old man, said to me. I had not asked her for her opinion. She was one of the invisible students in my home economics class. She knew how to make rice and beans and wasn't interested in the international dishes Señora Robles made us prepare, which would be useful for entertaining "your future husband's important guests." Lucila looked at movie magazines while the teacher talked, and wasn't reprimanded. She was one of those types of students in our school we knew as a different species: the girls, destined to marry young and bear many children who would go around barefoot in their seaside slums, and, as Abuela had pointed out, "swollen with bellies full of worms and parasites"; and the boys who would either perform menial services or hang around the plazas collecting American unemployment checks and harassing decent women with their *piropos*. Law forced the kids to stay in school until age sixteen, but it said nothing about anyone having to waste their energies on them. The teachers were our models for our interactions with polilla like Lucila. Not all of them were as snobbish as Mrs. Robles, though. She looked right through Lucila.

Señorita Vélez, on the other hand, actually visited these kids in their slum homes. One of her pet projects was to get more of them to finish high school so they'd have a chance at a different life from their parents'. She always reminded everyone in her Spanish literature and language classes that we didn't have to be like anyone else to be decent people. She challenged us to join in her mission, to visit the slums with her and see the reality of La Isla del Encanto for ourselves. For this vehemence she was ridiculed by most of her colleagues and by our parents, even though, since she was a Vélez, a member of one of the old Spanish families of San Juan, they nodded their heads when she spoke of her mission, and said, "*Sí, sí, señorita.*" But she remained alone in her efforts.

When even Miss Vélez began giving me the cold shoulder for what I assumed was my bad reputation, Lucila must have decided that I needed a friend, *any* friend. One day, as I was trying to ignore Lucila's attempts at conversation during recess, which I usually spent alone reading at the far end of the schoolyard, she leaned her face close to mine and hissed, "Next time pick a man, *un hombre,* niña. It'll make all the difference, I promise you. I mean señorita."

A wave of her cheap perfume hit me and made me nauseous. I gave her a dirty look and kept my eyes on my book. She smiled, showing a row of corn-yellow teeth—I recognized nicotine stains. It was a superior look she gave me. I began to hate her intensely then.

I wanted to, needed to, hate as much as possible. I hated Lucila for her presumptuousness. And I hated Wilhelm Lugar more than I hated anyone else. I let my hatred of him blossom like the overgrown water-swollen breadfruit that fell in our neighbor's backyard, exploding with a satisfying thud into a putrid white mush on the saturated ground. Before this hatred exploded, I had kept my eyes lowered when he was in the vicinity. I did my penance while he joked and laughed and passed notes to Marisa in our classes, letters that I suspected were about me.

But now I had a plan, one that meant alienating myself even more from my so-called friends, but I didn't care. I would soon disappear into a gray city like Patricio had done, maybe change my name too, change my life, and forget them all here on this claustrophobic island. I began to watch Wilhelm, to put myself obviously in his way, so that he had to walk around me in crowded hallways. I kept my eyes on him with such intensity that other students began teasing him that I was plotting his murder. People started watching me watch Wilhelm, pointing at us, so that Marisa could not get out of the spotlight if she wanted to be next to him.

Soon after, I heard that her parents had found out about their relationship. She would be attending an all-girls Catholic school the following year. The family could afford it now since their drugstore was driving the old-fashioned *farmacias* out of business. Marisa's brother Papito had been given the job of escorting her home every day until the end of school.

Wilhelm started missing shots at the games I faithfully attended. I arrived an hour early so I could wait near the players' door at the gym until he appeared with the team. The boys whistled at me, saying things that would have once humiliated me. But I didn't care. I wasn't invisible anymore, and Wilhelm, I suspected, was beginning to wish *he* were.

That year had been a nightmare, and in my recurring dream I was the pillager, conquering and burning the village, taking no hostages. But even as I lit the arrows and pulled the bowstring back painfully over my breasts, I knew that it was my own house that was in flames.

My mother was doing two things at once: she was packing everything she thought our family needed to take into "exile," as she referred to our imminent move, and she was also fighting the tide. She began to scan the classifieds for jobs in other towns that might entice my father. She'd tell him about hotels being built by American companies all over the island, the This and the That Inns. She was also looking for a cure from any source for Mili. Since the school was sending science to our house, my mother began to explore the realms of the mystical. After Papi dropped us off for the weekend at Abuela's, we'd visit religious shrines, consult old women about cures they had witnessed during their long lives, and talk, talk, talk with Abuela and my aunts about what Mamá Isadora would have done in such a situation.

I enjoyed the excursions to see places and people that would have enraged Papi, if he had known about them. He didn't want his daughters trained in the superstitious ways of so many island women, who believed they could change the natural course of events by wearing a coarse *penitente*'s habit for years as a *promesa*, a deal with God, giving up the pleasure of wearing nice clothes in exchange for divine favors. He thought this was really a childish idea about their power over forces they could not understand, much less change. He had forbidden Mami from committing herself to a year of wearing the blue-and-white raiment she had chosen, the colors of the Holy Mother, a deal she had struck with heaven in exchange for Mili's cure. My grandmother, for once, had agreed with him. She said wearing *hábitos* was for common women. But she did encourage my mother to visit the shrine of La Virgen de Monserrate in a small town near the west-coast city of Mayagüez. This was the site of a church-confirmed apparition of the Holy Mother.

And so we took a *público*, paid the driver too high a fare to drive us on a bumpy road lined with fields of sugarcane and rows of mango trees to the town dominated by a centuries-old church. My mother wore her black mantilla and Mili and I our white veils signifying our virginal unmarried status. Mili liked visiting new places though she acted as if we were tourists instead of *penitentes*, running from one thing to another as excited as a child at a carnival. My mother wanted to pray at the Stations of the Cross, which circled the hill where the church sat, each marked with a plaque, so that as you followed the path, you were climbing, like Jesus climbed to his crucifixion. As we approached the fifth station we came upon a life-size figure of Christ lying nearly naked on a stone tomb, red droplets of blood dripping from his wounds, coursing down his outstretched arms and across his flat belly. His eyes were closed and his mouth slightly open in a silent scream of agony. The sight seemed to excite Mili. Before we could hold her back, she had thrown herself on the lifelike marble figure. She laid her head on his chest and began sobbing violently. It took both Mami and me to pry her loose, but nothing we said to her—about it not being the real Jesus, only a statue—comforted her.

We finally persuaded her to calm down. But by the time we arrived at the sanctuary, where Mami hoped to pray in front of the statue of Mary, Mili would not stand still. She seemed to be over-whelmed by the thick atmosphere inside the Virgin's chapel: the profusion of votive candles burning in many colors, the cloud of incense from a censer a woman carried around the room, the body heat of the crowd pressed together and praying aloud in a holy babbling that surrounded us. When Mami pulled her toward Christ's mother, Mili began making choking sounds.

"What is it, Mili?" I put my arms around my sister, who was breathing hard and shaking as if she were about to have a seizure. Mami was determined to have her minute with *La Virgen* and I was trying to help her, though I feared that Mili might have to be carried out of this place that was upsetting her so much. "What is it, Mili? Tell me what's wrong."

"She let it happen, Consuelito. She let them do it to him."

"Who? What are you talking about, Mili?"

But she could hardly breathe, so I signaled to Mami that I was taking her outside. We sat on one of the marble benches along the atrium. I showed her how from there, the highest point in the town, we could see miles away to the green mountains. Mili slowly re-gained her color. I watched the people beginning to arrive for a Saturday night novena, noticing the looks my sister received from boys and men. She was beautiful, yet unaware of the body that was transforming her into a voluptuous woman from the neck down. Only her face remained as innocent as that of a five-year-old. It was hard to know what she was thinking, how she would react to any situation. I had to watch her constantly when we were around other people.

Strangely, the episode at the shrine brought on a period of calm for Mili. She spoke of wanting to live in a church, which Mami called a vocation, a miracle. Mili wanted to take the veil. Could this explain her specialness? My mother read about the lives of the visionary saints with a hunger that broke my heart. Saint Teresa of Ávila, the bride of Christ with her gift for verse, became her new patroness. Other members of the family were more skeptical.

"It's hormones, Angélica. Remember how I got really religious when I was about thirteen or fourteen?" Tía Awilda smiled enigmatically at her sisters. "But I was just confused about my feelings. After I met Rogelio, I knew it was not vocation for the veil that I had been experiencing."

"Awilda, have a little respect when you talk about the Church." It was Abuela who pursed her lips in my direction, indicating discretion was in order.

"He says we have to go by August, if we're going." My mother sounded tired. When she spoke, "he" always referred to my father. She was refusing to grant him the privilege of a name those days. "Domingo needs him to manage that *maldito* apartment building in Nueva Jersey *del diablo*, and the girls have to be enrolled in a school by September."

"You know they're talking about building a big resort hotel near here soon." Tía Divina was repeating something we had been hearing for years. The *autopista* that would connect the metropolitan areas of the island was going to open up possibilities for extending tourism from San Juan to the other coasts. No one knew, but many suspected, that it would be decades before the plan became a reality.

"Hija, I don't see that you have a choice," Abuela remarked sadly, rocking and fanning herself with an *abanico* from Spain she had inherited from her mother. "Mamá Isadora, who *hated* losing her girls to the Nueva York garment industry, still advised them to go if it was to save their marriages or to follow their husbands."

"*Ay bendito.*" Tía Divina lifted herself on her elbows from her reclining position on Abuela's sofa. She had recognized the sound of her husband's car approaching. "Why do we have to always do what *they* want?"

"That's the way it is, *querida.*" Abuela sighed, also rising. She went into her kitchen to start the ritual of *café colado*—boiling milk, straining it through a bleached muslin *colador*, and adding it to fresh-ground coffee. The women's meeting broke up as we all rearranged ourselves so that we weren't showing too much leg or sitting in a disrespectful position when Tío Yayo entered the room.

"What your family needs, Angélica," Tío Yayo said in his preaching voice—loud and dramatic—as he sat in Abuela's rocker waiting to be served his *café* and *pastelillos* by his wife, "is to take your daughters to church."

"We go to church, Agustín." My mother addressed him by his formal name, letting him know how much she resented his familiarity with her. She was about to utter her final *bueno*, when my uncle spoke the magic words to her.

"We have seen miracles happen at our services, *hermana.* Every week someone is healed through the power of El Señor working through our congregation. Bring your niña tonight. You will see that the evil that is dwelling in her soul will be eradicated by our prayers."

"*Bueno.*" The word came out of my mother's mouth with a wish clinging reluctantly to it. She looked at Abuela, who shrugged her shoulders. Who was she to deny her daughter a shred of hope, even if it involved participating in a rowdy Aleluya service? She'd have to endure the ridicule of her Catholic friends in the pueblo, but that was her price to pay.

Mami selected our most modest dresses, with long sleeves, high necks, and below-the-knee hemlines. She inspected our faces, particularly mine, for any traces of makeup, and had us put greasy dressing on our thick wild hair so it would lie down on our heads. The Pentecostal people liked to dress plainly. The Aleluya women never cut their hair but wore it in a tightly wound bun at their napes. No lipstick, no high heels, no loud colors, no dancing. Abuelo said that the Pentecostals were part of the foreign conspiracy to change the Puerto Rican character: When had there ever been a Puerto Rican who did not enjoy music? It was in our national soul. He told his indifferent audience at home about a religious sect in America who had said no to everything including sex, and guess what? They had died out in one generation!

Abuela had muttered something about it not being such a bad idea. *La religión* had saved one of her daughters' marriages; it had rescued a man from *el ron*. So she no longer closed her doors when the plain women came around distributing their pamphlets printed on cheap newsprint that would yellow on her coffee table in days, and soon line her parakeet's cage.

We marched ourselves to their current church, an old house in town where several times a week folding chairs would be set up in rows for a congregation of about two dozen faithful who brought their tambourines and sang their songs so loudly I had always thought they numbered in the hundreds. They were already into their first number when we came in. Mili was acting skittish so we sat in the back row. Prepared to be bored out of my head, I actually found myself swaying to the infectious rhythms of a hymn, sung with such energy that the wood floor was shaking. Abuelo had been wrong about the Aleluyas being music-deprived. They seemed to have adopted the *clave*, the three-beat rhythm of our popular music, into their praises of El Señor.

We sat with Mili between us in a row of swaying chairs. At the peak of the service a heavy woman, sweating profusely, rose abruptly, toppling her chair back into our laps, and began to testify passionately. She begged the Lord to purge evil from this congregation. With shouted aleluyas other people joined her in calling out their supplications to the Lord. Mili seemed to become agitated in the midst of the confusion of voices and the waving of arms by a congregation now infused with the Holy Spirit. Her voice startled me as it rose above the others in an unintelligible rush of words. She jumped up from her seat with a look of ecstasy on her face, her arms waving in a perfect imitation of the fat lady. Everyone turned to stare at us and soon only Mili's passionate shouts in an incomprehensible language echoed off the zinc roof of that old house. Mami was trying to restrain her. I grasped Mili's hand, but her strength defeated us both. Tío Yayo had taken the microphone again and was calling her forward.

"This niña is in touch with God. She is speaking to us in a divine tongue. Let her come forward."

"Aleluya! Aleluya!" The congregation only needed to be told once how to react. I knew that if Tío had said my sister was possessed by demons, they would have believed him too. But Tío's voice had an immediate effect on Mili. Instead of rushing forward, she turned and ran out the door with Mami and me in pursuit.

Mami was devastated and, worse, defeated. When Papi arrived that Sunday night to pick us up, she had returned his given name to him.

"Carlos," she said once we were in the car, in the new rueful voice she would use for a long time to come, "it's time to buy our airline tickets, while you are still getting a paycheck."

Papi gently pulled her head to his shoulder, and she didn't resist; she slept or pretended to sleep during most of the trip home.

What followed was the eye of the storm, a period of calm, a time when music returned to our house and my mother seemed to regain some of her sense of fun. Nothing had been solved, but Mili's illness was now a part of our lives. It was like a trial period to see if we could still function as a family. Mami turned on the radio again, as if to drown out any disturbing thoughts. She bought the albums of that tormented singer Daniel Santos, a lost soul whose voice was like a lament by someone who had visited hell and come back to tell us about it. He sang like a fallen angel, Mami said.

Papi brought out his old guitar and began playing it again at night. But there were no words to the melodies he played. I could hear them from my room, where I spent a lot of time reading, and the way he lingered over some chords, it seemed that he wanted the guitar to speak. Images came to my mind as I listened to Papi's compositions. I assumed they were his creations, as I had never heard the music before, and I wondered whether he was singing quietly while he played. What were his songs about? His dream of being a professional songwriter was supposedly dead, but now he seemed unable to stay away from his guitar for long. Sometimes he played for Mili, whose eyes turned up in that look of religious ecstasy that always made me think of Saint Teresa's Passion, as it was illustrated in our Catholic book of saints and martyrs.

On a good day when Papi was singing for Mili, and all seemed calm, my mother announced that she and I were going to the beauty shop. Since I was tired of the house, I agreed to the unexpected offer.

The surprise was that we took the bus to El Condado with my mother acting suspiciously giddy, as if we were schoolgirls playing hooky.

"Where are we going?" I asked for the third time, as we got off the bus and continued walking in the direction of the beach and the ritziest of the Condado hotels.

"You will see, hija." She had the mischievous smile that I had not seen on her face for a long time.

We walked into the lobby of the huge Queen of the Sea, a hotel recently renovated to resemble a luxury ocean liner. The staff all wore maritime uniforms with epaulets and captain's hats, the windows were portholes, and the color scheme was a dizzying variation of blues. There was even the sound of crashing waves coming from speakers hidden behind decorative life preservers.

"Ugh." I had had enough training in architectural beauty from Patricio to be repelled by the Hollywood-inspired snazziness of the place. "Mami, what are we doing here?"

"*Ven.*" My mother linked arms with me and led me down the thickly carpeted corridor of the lobby. It featured the souvenir shops, shoeshine stand, and other hotel services, all, of course, done in the theme of great steam liners of the past with maritime artifacts in every shape and form—anchor ashtrays, sextant clocks, porthole wall mirrors—and employees in white uniforms and epaulets at every corner. We came to the beauty shop whose window was framed in seaweed garlands.

"*Mira*, Consuelo."

I gasped in amazement. Sitting behind a vanity table shaped like a carved mermaid holding up a gilt-framed mirror was . . . María Sereno! He was dressed in a white cabin mate's parade uniform with huge shoulder decorations of braids and fringe. His chest was flat but covered in medals and ribbons. He looked stunning. Although he was busily buffing an elegantly dressed woman's nails, he saw us and waved happily, motioning for us to come in.

"Mami?" I was puzzled. Why were we here?

"Consuelo, María Sereno and his mother have been a comfort to me during these past months. Don't look so shocked. Am I not allowed to have my little secrets too?"

"I never saw them around."

"I visited with them when you were in school. He has a special touch with Mili, you know. Some days I just could not stay alone with your sister. Let's go in. I made us manicure appointments."

"How long has he been working here?"

"Not too long. He got the job through one of the nurses at the hospital where he was when . . . when he had the fall . . . *tu sabes*. Her sister is a hairstylist here. He is doing so well, Consuelo. The tourists just love him."

Seeing that we weren't coming in, María Sereno came to us. He took my hands in his, smiled, and pronouncing them "*Un desastre, mi amor*," led us to his mermaid table.

We did not talk of our troubles that afternoon. María Sereno entertained the whole place with hilarious stories of the foreign women whose hands he worked on. And in his cuentos the bizarre became so common that I expressed disbelief out loud, and he said to me that I had not been looking closely enough, or I would have known by now that being "normal" is a rare thing. We laughed until we had tears running down our faces at the things he told us. And when we stepped outside the Queen of the Sea, I felt slightly seasick, as if I had really been away on a cruise. María Sereno had pinned one of his medals on my blouse, a memento, he called it. It was a bronze star. I thought it was a fake, but had to think quickly when, as soon as we got home, my father asked me where I had gotten it.

"I found it on the bus," I told him.

"It's a medal for courage in the field of action. Strange that someone would be carrying it around with him."

"Or with *her*." My mother threw the words at us as she hurried to check on Mili, whom my father was obviously not watching closely.

My own alternate life of plotting vengeance against my enemies was less lyrical than my parents' retreat into their musical fantasies. It was the narrative poem of war I was composing, in the style of Homer, adding stanzas each day. I was not Penelope though, but Odysseus planning the climax of my own epic.

I had this idea that I had awakened Wilhelm to his real nature, and now he hated me for it. He was not really a man, just a little boy who took what he wanted, then ran away. I had also discovered something important about myself—I had a secret life that no one knew about. In my mind I began to plan Wilhelm's punishment, while on the outside I continued to be the good daughter, Consuelo.

I relished the secret I kept from my family about my lost virginity. I knew the explosive power of what I had done; exposure would mean a mere slap on the wrist for Wilhelm, but a *tragedia* for my parents. I imagined scenarios in which I was cast out on the streets and had to become a prostitute in San Juan because no *hombre decente* would touch me. In my fantasy though, unlike the *perdidas* in real life, I would make a fortune by selling my body to *los americanos* who stayed at El San Juan Hotel, where they played for high stakes in the casino. Papi had said that was all these men saw of the island; then they'd go back to their mainland suburbs and say that Puerto Rico was nothing but thieves and whores.

As rebellious as I was feeling, even the revised version of my daydream did not really convince me. I was scared, actually, prey to a growing feeling of panic, as if I had planted a bomb in my own house and now minutes were ticking off until the explosion. By the week of final exams, I was ready to get on that Pan Am airbus, ready to fall out of the sky into a concrete-and-steel box of a city where I would feel safe again. In another version of my dream, I found Patricio in a crowd in this unknown city and followed him to a beautiful place, a secret garden, where every flower was special because he had nurtured it. And there nothing evil could enter— not madness, not gossip, not desire for anything but beauty. And nothing and no one could hurt us—for it would be a sealed garden, like Eden.

The AVE MARÍA and Other Flightless Birds

Patricio wrote less and less frequently. By the time we began our last summer on the island, I was getting an occasional note from "Patty Swan." He had been promoted to personal assistant to the famous designer. His friend, the one who had introduced him to the designer, was not mentioned after a while. On weekends, Patricio was now staying in his boss's country home in Vermont, helping him renovate an old house. Patricio said he felt like a child in Disneyland. He was given all the money he wanted to spend on art supplies, material, and furniture. Most of my cousin's letters were about the startling natural beauty of the state, green like our island, and mountainous, but more pure in its topography, he said, as if God had taken his time planning it. This northern place was an elegant land, no abrupt shifts from wet to dry and high to low as in our little country, which, like our mothers' houses, was crammed with too many decorations.

The new sophisticated and critical Patricio did not ask about my life, though I had been writing to him about Mili's deteriorat-

ing condition and about our urgent desire to have real lives again. I
told him that I would enjoy seeing New York City in his company.
I wanted to experience it as we had Old San Juan, to meet his fascinating friends—the painters, the designers he spoke of in his letters. But Patricio made no reply to my written wishes and hints. We
seemed to be corresponding in two different languages, and I could
only hope that he would include me in his life once we arrived in
New York. Tío Domingo was still holding on to his apartment
building in New Jersey where we would live. Using a map in the
Britannica, I measured the distance between where we'd be and
New York City: a long way by island standards, but no more than
from San Juan to my grandparents' pueblo.

I occupied myself during these last weeks by helping my
mother decide what to take and what to leave behind. Papi passed
by our piles and would often say, "Throw that away. They'll have
something better where we're going." But Mami kept the things she
wanted whether he pronounced them obsolete or not: the muslin
colador, hand sewn by Abuela to make *café con leche*; the heavy
ollas, the cast-iron pots and pans that had belonged to Mamá
Isadora; the set of unbreakable tableware to which Mami had
grudgingly become attached, since she could throw dishes and cups
into her sink from any point in her kitchen in a gesture of defiance
she seemed to enjoy.

In contrast, I tried to give away everything of my past life.
I only wanted my books, but I was made to choose just a few.
Mami's *ollas* had used up most of our weight limit. So I had to
leave my encyclopedia at Abuela's house, where it would become a
part of Abuelo's library. He had reluctantly agreed to place the
English-language books in a bookcase across the room from his
beloved volumes. Everyone joked that he secretly feared the American books would corrupt his Puerto Rican literature; or maybe the
volumes would mate during the night. Then he'd have to deal with

the polyglot language of the illegitimate offspring, a fate worse than death to his purist soul. Jokes aside, Abuelo was grieving over our family's decision to leave.

"I fear I may never see you again, hija." He stood in the doorway of his library watching me arrange the *Britannica* in alphabetical order the day I brought the books to his house. I had to smile. He sounded like a trained actor when he spoke. I came over to him and wrapped my arms around his stout middle. Dressed in his tan linen suit, holding his Panama hat in his hand, he looked as if he were posing for a formal portrait. His dark skin was still practically unlined, and his thick cap of glossy black hair had only a little diadem of silver around the edges framing his dignified face. His large features were like those of the bust of a Roman senator I had seen in a picture. But Abuelo's eyes were Indian, slightly slanted, and his pupils and irises were black, a rare and beautiful thing according to a popular song I had heard, *ojos negros, piel canela*, eyes of black, cinnamon skin, Puerto Rican beauty. Abuelo kissed my forehead tenderly. I hugged him tight.

"We will see you often, *Abuelito*. It's easy to take an airplane; we can come home anytime we want. And you can come visit us."

"No, niña. You don't understand. I have sworn in front of God and man that I would never set foot in the land of our invaders. As for you coming home, the place will not let you return, not really. If you do come home, you will no longer be the same. I have seen the changes in the ones who go there . . ."

I didn't let him go on with his lament, which was likely to turn into an impassioned sermon. Instead I kissed his cheek. I knew my grandfather had a heart and head full of beautiful ideas about our island. His lifelong study of poems and great literature had made him fall in love with our country as if it were a woman. He spoke about cherishing *la isla*, protecting it, loving it. He spoke of it in the terms a lover uses to talk about his beloved.

He handed me a small package wrapped in brown paper and tied with a string.

"Food for your Puerto Rican soul, hija. You are like me, a lover of the word."

What Abuelo gave me was three books from his collection. Old books beautifully bound in cloth and leather, the spines cracked from so much use: *The Indian Legends of Puerto Rico and the Caribbean*, the book of folk music and old hymns I had once borrowed, and a collection of cuentos, folktales, ghost stories, proverbs, and *adivinanzas*, the riddles everyone told and retold until we all knew the answers and had learned how to improvise funny new ones.

"Tell me, Doña Awilda, the name of the bird that isn't made of flesh and blood and doesn't need wings to fly to heaven?" our uncle might ask with pretend seriousness of his angry wife.

"The *Ave María*, you fool," she might answer, unable to suppress a smile. "And you should be getting quite a few Hail Marys to say or to pluck next time you go to confession as punishment for your load of sins," she might retort, turning the pun on him.

Our family had words for every occasion, even pain and sorrow. The ones my mother started quoting in those final days on the island, as if she needed a prefabricated explanation for our family's dilemma, were all fatalistic: "Each hour that passes wounds us, the last one kills us." Or "Death kills you only once, but you die little by little all your life."

I looked to my books for hope. Poetry only confirmed what my mother's proverbs warned me about: life was a struggle, with only an occasional hard-earned glimpse of beauty as a reward. And worse, love did not always equal beauty. Only the truth mattered, proclaimed the poets, but it too, if you ever discovered it, almost inevitably brought pain. At least that's what Julia de Burgos, my Julia, and Sorrowful Lady of my Dark Nights, told me through her sad, haunting verses.

I studied picture books about northern cities, to see if I could learn to find beauty in a place that was soon to be my home. The gray buildings and crowded streets no longer seemed as unappealing when I traced their sharp geometric outlines with my eyes and my fingers on the glossy pages of my books. There was some comfort in the monochromatic shadows and designs of American cities, in the patterns one could rearrange and interpret.

It must have been then, at the end of my last year of being an island Puerto Rican—a status that, as my grandfather warned me, once surrendered one can never reclaim—that I began to understand that words were the key to power and freedom. That was why Patricio had mastered English, in preparation for his escape, and why Abuelo guarded his books like a dragon sitting on treasure—his library was his secret source of wealth. But I wondered about Mili, who still often retreated to her own world. She hid in that place where we couldn't reach her with our Spanish words. The psychologist had called it schizophrenia, a label my father had rejected in anger. Papi had railed at the mild-mannered young graduate of the University of Puerto Rico, saying he was a badly educated phony whose credentials would never stand up to American standards. Papi's plan was to get Mili to some "real" doctors in New York. He was convinced that there was some pill or medicine, simply not available on the island, that would restore his pretty daughter to her former vivacious, social self. My mother and I had learned to remain silent when Papi's despair took him into the fantasyland of a North American paradise. He was no fool, but he was in pain, as we all were, and grasping for any way of dealing with it.

I had my lust for revenge and my secrets to sustain me. I had experienced the pleasure of having been begged by Wilhelm to suspend my silent stalking of him, which had brought him the kind of attention he had tried desperately to avoid. I still carried his note in my purse, and I occasionally brought it out to remind me of how unimportant he had become.

Please, Consuelo. Stop prosecuting me. I don't love you. I'm Marisa's boyfriend now. He had meant to write "persecuting" of course, probably to impress me with his English. But he was just proving that he was not really bilingual. Forgetting his English as he replaced it with Spanish, he was now simply bad at two languages.

But it had been *el relajo*, the scorn and mockery of his former friends, that had brought him to his knees. From stardom on the court, he had fallen into the humiliating role of rejected suitor of Marisa, and also of possibly being my despoiler. I had become a figure everyone in our culture recognized, *la sufrida*. My family was going through a *tragedia*, as everyone knew, and here was this outsider, the absurdly named Wilhelm, who mangled the Spanish language, who had damaged one *puertorriqueña* and was trying to get his hands on the best catch in the school, Marisa Morales. Of course what had clinched it was that Wilhelm's game had really begun to suffer. It was lack of concentration, the boys said; it was a guilty conscience, the girls countered. I remained poignantly silent in the last bleacher at the top.

Toward the end of the season I got a note from Wilhelm asking me to meet him at a new hamburger joint in the city. I went, of course, dressed in an immaculate white skirt and blouse, looking like I was going to make my First Communion or take my vows. I told the one girl at school who was still speaking to me—mainly to get gossip to feed the others—about the rendezvous. This girl was known behind her back as La Telefónica, because if you wanted something to get around school, all you had to do was let *la bomba* drop within her hearing. Her gossip network extended far and wide.

I was not surprised to find Pedro's Burger crammed with people who normally would have avoided the place. Wilhelm was crouched in a back booth pretending to be totally involved in reading the one-page menu. I squared my shoulders and held my head in the style of María Sereno as I walked in. There were murmurs and a few giggles, but I looked neither right nor left, just straight ahead. It was *my* show. Although I was lifted by my own bravura, I could also practically smell the fire consuming the last footbridge home. Or maybe it was the grease on Pedro's grill assailing my nostrils and giving me a queasy stomach.

Sliding into the red vinyl seat across from Wilhelm, I was aware of all the eyes upon us. I folded my hands on the table, acting the part of the demure señorita for all it was worth. I glanced around once to see amused but not hostile faces witnessing my one-act play. Wilhelm kept his shoulders hunched as though he wanted to hide his head inside himself like a turtle.

"Consuelo, you have to stop it." He kept his voice low and his eyes averted toward the wall.

"Stop what, Wilhelm? I do not understand you." We were speaking in English, his best language, which gave me the advantage of protesting ignorance of his words at will.

"You do know what I'm talking about. You've ruined everything for me here."

"I've done what?" I let my voice rise and he crunched down even more in his seat. There were giggles from the other tables.

"What do you want me to do, Consuelo?"

"Tell everyone that you lied about me."

"I can't do that. You know what you did." Wilhelm was turning deep red under his brown skin, as if the memory of making love to me was too shameful a thing to put into words. I laughed at his accusation of what *I* had done—as though he had played no part in the act. It was just as I had heard all my life: a girl has to take the blame if she and a man have sex together. Only *she* is at fault for the sin. After all, men have no control over their sexual desires. I was determined to test this truism.

"You asked me a question, I have answered it."

"But you are leaving soon. What does it matter what people say?"

"You don't understand, dear Wilhelm. It's not because it matters to others that I want you to do this. I just want to see if it works. I want to see if gossip can change my life again, even a little. I want to know if *el chisme* has a reverse gear."

"You want me to tell people that I lied about you? You are strange, Consuelo."

"Maybe I am, Wilhelmcito. But I have the power now, don't I? That's why you're here, no?"

Obviously in a rage, he leaped from the booth and rushed out of the restaurant to a trail of murmurs and giggles. I made a big show of paying for his Coke. There was a little riff of applause from one of the groups, but I didn't turn to look. I walked out with my new attitude wrapped around me like a silk shawl from Spain.

There had not been enough time before the end of school for the scheme to really take effect, but Wilhelm had tried to appease me. And I had received an anonymous note saying that several of the girls in my class believed I had been "wronged" by that polilla, Wilhelm. They had wished me luck in *los Estados*. I had thanked him for his efforts by not attending an exhibition game where he had managed to play almost up to his old standards.

Finally, it didn't really matter what people thought about me. When it was over I realized that it had been only a means of keeping my mind occupied (with other things besides our family's problems), and learning how to manage my loneliness as my world was being dismantled and put in boxes. I felt like one of the women on the first ships to the New World. I imagined some of them must have wrapped up a few loose ends before sailing into the unknown, must have done a few things that they did not plan to regret.

But it was to be my sometime nemesis, Miss Vélez, who would provide me with a final vision of *La Isla*, one that would change me forever. And I had almost missed my chance. I had put off the required Survey of Literature and Culture class until my senior year. Miss Vélez was reputed to make her course as hard as possible for students who resisted joining her political causes. But once in her class, I felt compelled by her passionate lectures on "understanding ourselves by exploring our island, both its beauty and its ugliness." I accepted Miss Vélez's challenge to her students—*to see the other side of our little island for yourself.* Having made my decision in arrogance, I had not expected La Perla to affect me the way it did. It would be a revelation I would carry with me always, along with the vision of my Isla del Encanto.

Intensely curious about Señorita Vélez, I had dropped her name into a conversation with my mother at the first opportunity. We had been running to get the dry clothes off the line before an *aguacero*. For the first time in many days, my mother had laughed as we raced against the black clouds rolling in, fat as pregnant cows, she had said, with bursting teats.

In the kitchen we sat down to black coffee, and she to her ever-present cigarette. She suddenly asked me if I had a love interest.

"*¿No hay novios?*" She had smiled conspiratorially at me across the shiny green Formica separating us. "No boyfriends in sight?"

I shrugged, neither confirming nor denying.

"I don't want any *jamonas* in our family, Consuelito."

"Like Miss Vélez?" I made my voice sound like hers, slightly mocking, encouraging, but not so interested that she might suspect my real motives.

"Hmm. *La Vélez* may have had a more interesting past than most of us know."

"What do you mean?"

"*No sé.* I really don't know all the details. But the rumor is that her family, the very proper *familia Vélez y Vélez*, had their lovely daughter 'finish her education' in *los Estados Unidos* because she was pregnant."

"That's probably just *el chisme*, Mami. She's a good person." I hadn't meant to jump in and defend my teacher, but the wagging tongues of San Juan were known to start flapping as soon as a woman went anywhere on her own. My mother raised her eyebrows. I had given myself away. She crushed her cigarette on the ashtray and shrugged, obviously mocking my coyness.

"*Bueno.*" She rubbed her hands together as if washing herself free of *other* people's sins. "*Pues, no sé.* I just know that when she came back there were no more offers of marriage."

"So why didn't she marry the father of her child?"

"He disappeared, niña. All I know was that he was a man from La Perla. Her family would have probably had him castrated so he couldn't defile any more of their porcelain señoritas."

Miss Vélez's story had now fallen into another category—the

parable of the fallen woman—and I no longer trusted it to be the truth. So, more out of curiosity about Miss Vélez's fascinating secret past life than out of missionary zeal to see the *other* Puerto Rico, I was ready to spend time with my teacher.

The night before my excursion with Miss Vélez, I had told Mami that I was being given a going-away party by my schoolmates at the beach. I planned to be at the curb waiting for Miss Vélez's Ford station wagon to pull up so as not to give my parents a chance to talk to her. They would, I hoped, assume that she was driving me there.

I had had a dream that night that I was alone in a forest, hypnotically drawn to a fire burning its way out toward the houses in the distance. I felt its warmth as I approached and had a strong desire to be completely enveloped by it. I walked into the flames at the center but was not consumed; instead, I was bathed by its radiance. Emerging on the other side, I could see that it was not a raging fire but a column of flames. It was contained and beautiful. There was no danger of it spreading to the houses. As I was about to walk through the pleasant heat again, back to the other side, I heard my mother calling me from far away. I turned toward her voice, but the columns had closed in like a firewall, scorching my hands when I tried to push through to where I thought she was.

That is when I was awakened by the sounds of my family. I heard music in Mili's room. That meant that she was having a good day. And from the kitchen came the plastic clacking of dishes being set out on the Formica table. Mami called my name. It was time to get up and get ready for my farewell party.

The shantytown of La Perla sits by the sea at the bottom of the ancient wall of the old city of San Juan. It is both ugly and beautiful.

I had seen its crazy outline of rusted zinc rooftops from the road. To get into the barrio one had to go through a little tunnel dug out of the fort wall. Miss Vélez maneuvered her car to the side of the road and parked it. Then she placed a sign on the inside of the windshield that read OFFICIAL BUSINESS. I got out when she did, following her through the sudden darkness of the damp-smelling cavern and back out into the blinding light of midmorning. We found ourselves on a cement slab with a couple of benches on it.

"Your tour starts here, Consuelo. Try to understand that it took me a couple of years to develop the trust of the people here. I hope that you will keep this important fact in mind today: we are not here to pass judgment. Try not to be shocked by the language you'll hear. The residents of La Perla do not censor their speech like you and I do—maybe that makes them a bit more honest. What do you think?" She smiled down at me.

"I'm not a child, or a prude, Señorita Vélez."

"I know you are not a child, señorita." She shot the word back at me. I could see the day with Miss Vélez wasn't going to be a picnic at the beach.

As we stood in the plaza of La Perla trying to adjust to the bright sun, I saw that we were not alone. In fact it seemed that every house held several pairs of eyes trained on us. In a couple of doorways, there were little children hanging on to women's skirts. Most of the toddlers were barefoot and barely clothed in panties or a pair of shorts. One naked boy took his tiny penis in his hands and aimed a stream of urine in our direction. Of course it missed, but his intention was obvious and soon there was laughter, and comments were shouted at him.

"¡Mira! That *machito* is already taking aim at the ladies, Clara! You better watch out for him!" an older woman called out in the direction of the little boy's mother.

"Well, he can wait a few years to get fresh with the women. He is a little devil, this one."

"Clara, don't take the boy's pride away from him. He's just showing what he's got."

A man with his shirt flapping open over a bare chest waved a brown beer bottle at the women. "I could come over and show his mami what I've got!"

"No thank you, Berto, that's how I got my little *diablo* in the first place. I already know what I need to know about what men have to offer," Clara answered, patting her swollen belly. There was more laughter and then a general shuffling as people returned to what they were doing before they had noticed the outsiders on the plaza.

I had been startled by the open and unabashed exchange I had just witnessed. My mother and her sisters bantered about sexual matters, but their words were always masked in subtle references, at least while the children were around. These people had simply said whatever came into their heads aloud, in front of anyone. I must have been blushing because I turned to see Miss Vélez smiling sarcastically at me.

"Are you sure this isn't going to be too much for you, Consuelo?"

I didn't answer but walked ahead on a path leading down toward the center of the barrio. The bricks and stones were worn smooth as mirrors by centuries of use, and the sky was reflected in them. We followed the trail onto the ledge by the sea that was called La Perla. A tepid sea breeze carried the smell of the open sewage that ran through this place as well as the fragrance of the many flowering trees and shrubs growing among rusted automobiles and discarded appliances. Modern art, I thought, like in the catalogues Patricio had ordered from museums in New York, places he told me he would one day see for himself.

Through the shacks stacked haphazardly in layers, I got glimpses of a turquoise sea streaked in aquamarine, lines of refuse rocking in its currents. Coming nearer to a *cuartel*, a cement-block building of three apartments, I heard several radios blasting out the same song, a merengue that kept urging, "Shake it, baby, shake it, 'cause the sugar is at the bottom." A heavy woman was sweeping piles of sand out of her *cuartel* and moving her large hips to the wild rhythms of the music. When she saw us she dropped her broom and ran toward Miss Vélez. The women embraced enthusiastically. I had never seen Miss Vélez so animated. She and the woman talked nonstop for a few minutes, having apparently forgotten about me. I sat on a cement block in front of the *cuartel*, taking shallow breaths because the sewage odors had gotten more intense as we neared the houses.

"Consuelo Signe, this is Doña Rosario."

I rose. "*Mucho gusto, Señora.*"

"Please, don't *doña* or *señora* me and I won't *señorita* you. *¿De acuerdo?*"

I looked at Miss Vélez, who just smiled. I was on my own.

"Consuelo, you know this lady's daughter. She's your classmate."

"Lucila?" There was a resemblance.

Miss Vélez nodded. I was amazed. This woman didn't look old enough to have a daughter my age; she was perhaps in her late twenties or early thirties. There was also a little girl leaning out of the door of her *cuartel* who couldn't have been more than two years old.

"Come in. Come in. Let's have some *café*. Lucila should be home from her job in San Juan any time now. She'll be glad to see you."

"Where does Lucila work, Rosario?" Miss Vélez entered the apartment without glancing back at me.

"She works three nights a week at the Grand Beach Hotel. Goes in at midnight, gets off at eight. It's pretty good money for washing glasses at the bar."

I was still sitting on the cement block when I saw Lucila walking down the cobblestone path. I hardly recognized her in her white kitchen-worker's uniform, her hair pulled back in a bun; but it was how tired she looked that shocked me. As she got closer, I could see dark rings around her eyes. Makeup streaked by sweat gave her face a hardened look. She had obviously worked a shift and a half since it was past noon already. When she saw me she put her hands on her hips, shook her head, and laughed harshly.

"Are you writing a report for school, señorita, or taking a survey? How can we help you?"

"I'm here with Miss Vélez," I answered, embarrassed at the memory of having snubbed Lucila after the Wilhelm episode. How could Miss Vélez do this to me? I considered walking away. I had money in my pocket and could get out to the road and take a *público* home. *If* public cars ever came out here.

I felt Lucila's eyes on me, but I wouldn't look at her.

"Why don't you get off your butt before it gets a callus from that hard block, and come inside for a cup of coffee, señorita? I'm dying for some."

I looked up to see Lucila's weary face transformed by an amused smile. She handed me the small bag of groceries she had been carrying, and picked up the little girl who had run out to greet her.

"Come here, my *bebita*." She cradled the little girl in her arms. "Has my *nena* been an angel or a devil with Abuelita today?"

The coffee seemed to revive Lucila. She asked me if I wanted to walk down to the beach where she said a house had been struck by lightning recently. There was something there she wanted; her mother seemed to know what it was.

"Bring me one, Lucila. Make sure it hasn't been touched by anyone else."

We slid down the steep hillside where the boxy houses sat on thin stilts like women holding up their skirts to cross a puddle, brown women with skinny legs wearing pastel colors. I spoke this aloud without thinking. My fanciful image made Lucila laugh.

"Is that what you do with your time, niña, think of pretty words to describe ugly things?" I nearly tumbled down a slippery hillside strewn with litter. Lucila put her arm around my waist to steady me. She smelled strongly of the cheap perfume I had identified on her once before, and of sweat. But it was not an affront out here, in this strange place where everything smelled of garbage and the sea, of sewage and perfumed ocean breezes. The tide was low and I saw that there were glittering things embedded in the sand, shiny colorful little jewels sparkling in the sun: rubies, emeralds, and diamonds. I picked one up. Broken bottle glass worn smooth by the surf. I looked back and saw the wobbly birthday cake of La Perla, almost pretty with the sun casting a golden glow over the shacks. The houses were either unpainted wood, cement *cuarteles*, or single homes of parakeet yellow, pink, and various hues of green and blue. Many of them had TV antennae sticking crookedly this way and that on the different levels of tarpaper roofs. This was architecture Patricio should have seen. I would have liked for him to try sketching La Perla.

The place seemed to throb with the communal energy of many people crowded into small places. The music from doorways and windows blended into a sort of engine hum. I felt as though the entire barrio might rise like a giant spaceship and take off over the water. Encouraged by Lucila's friendly laughter, I told her what I was thinking.

"*Ay*, Consuelo. Sometimes I wish I could take off over this ocean, like those *garzas* over there, and see what the rest of the world looks like. But you are crazy, *loca*, if you think I want to take all these bums with me!" She swept her arm over La Perla and the seagulls circling above us. Though still wearing her kitchen-worker's uniform, Lucila was barefoot and I saw that she had opened several buttons at her neck. The weariness I had been shocked to see earlier seemed to be easing out of her solid body, especially when she smiled and waved to her neighbors, or when she winked at the boy who whistled at us, telling us he had a boat nearby and that we could take a cruise with him. Other times, like when I asked her about her job, Lucila's shoulders sagged.

"Señorita Vélez wants me to finish high school. But I don't know if I can do it. Mami can't work. She's sick. A female problem that gets really bad when she's on her feet too long. You know, it's rough without a man bringing in a paycheck. I'm getting married next month. My baby's father. He's no saint, but better than no man at all. He's got a good job at the marina."

"What happened to your father?"

"My father didn't stay around long enough to see if his seed had taken root!" Lucila laughed.

I probably seemed embarrassed, because she took my hand and steered me toward a pile of singed wood that must have once been a house. I saw patches of pink on some of the boards. It was evident from the stacking of some cement blocks and piles of rocks on either side of the ruins that it had been picked through. Lucila crouched to examine the piles carefully.

"What are you looking for, Lucila?" I could not see anything of value or use in the rubble.

"I'm looking for a little gift from the god of thunder, Changó."

She used a stick to pull a sooty stone out of the pile.

"This is a thunderstone. Very powerful magic, if no one has touched it. You can tell because it doesn't have any marks on the soot, see? It will still have Changó's power in it."

"What do you use it for?" I was glad I wasn't totally ignorant about Santeria rituals. I had read in Abuelo's books about the African religions brought to the Caribbean by the slaves. But I hadn't heard of thunderstones.

"We keep them in a *batea* at home. I'll show you. They bring good luck to the house."

"That's not all you do with them, is it?"

"Maybe not, Consuelito. But the rest may be too shocking for your virgin ears." She winked at me, smiling. I knew about the animal sacrifices of Santeria rituals and I knew that they were not discussed with outsiders like me. Yet I could not help feeling left out again. There was always something someone would not say in front of me. But I also knew the power of secrets. They were not to be easily given away. So I winked back at Lucila and asked no more questions.

Lucila took my hand as we walked back to her house. She began singing a verse of "Verde Luz" that I knew, and I joined her. Even in this place made ugly by poverty, our island could not stop being praised for its beauty.

On the way home Miss Vélez hardly stopped talking about the government's disgraceful indifference toward La Perla and about how we were all accomplices. Every other sentence was punctuated with an emotional *¡Ave María!*

I said nothing. The raw misery and startling beauty I found among the ruins of La Perla had made me feel the sort of yearning sadness, *la tristeza*, that our poets and composers tried to put into words and music, that Abuelo struggled to articulate. *El amor.* I recognized it now. It was love I felt for my island, as well as a fear of being blinded by it.

And Some Songs of EL AMOR

There was little laughter at Abuela's house in the last weeks before our departure. My mother was accorded the respectful treatment owed her, *la sufrida*. She was treated as if she were carrying too heavy a load to be able to rise from her chair for a cigarette or a cup of coffee. Mili stayed indoors close to Mami, afraid of losing sight of her. Her counselor had suggested that drawing might keep Mili focused and calm, and so Papi had bought her a sketch pad and pencils. She seemed to have an eye for details, she found the key to someone's face, hands, eyes, especially the eyes, and zoomed in on it. She sat on the floor drawing amazingly accurate pencil caricatures of us, never saying a word. It was not always pleasing to see ourselves exposed in her art, but criticism didn't penetrate the self-absorbed haze Mili inhabited. She studied her drawings, like a psychologist reading her notes after a session with a patient, and then set them aside as soon as she made whatever discovery it was she was after.

I had begun keeping the discarded pages in a folder. I felt that the drawings were another medium of communication for Mili, that she was learning something about people's minds from her study of their exteriors. I envied her gift. I would have liked to capture Lucila's essence in a sketch: Lucila the chameleon, the Madonna of La Perla, who could turn from a young girl into a tired old woman and back according to the demands of her chaotic world. And the tough *jamona*, Miss Vélez, whose eyes got moist and her cheeks pink when the child at Lucila's house climbed on her lap and went to sleep holding on to her—because she liked the way the teacher smelled of candy, she had said.

In Mili's drawing, Papi's eyes were turned away, facing the edge of the frame, above him a cloud-filled sky; Mami's were turned down toward her feet, coming to a point like a spike hammered into the ground. It was a peculiarity of Mili's sketches that the faces loomed like huge balloons over tiny bodies. It was the face that interested Mili, and she caught something that was true for each person she drew: the scowl, the smirk, the tender smile. Mami could not stand to look at them, and I understood the fear they must have inspired in her—but they seemed, somehow, exactly right. Once I watched Mami reluctantly examine the portrait of Papi, perhaps because she needed to see how he appeared to others, or perhaps she was looking for clues, as always, of his betrayals. But all she saw was a surreal version of her husband, gazing dreamily at clouds, looking for something Mili would not reveal to us. Mami was about to crumple up the drawing when I took it from her hands. I wanted to save it for later, when I could read it like a book.

"I don't know what good it does her to make these silly doodlings. Do you?"

She released the paper to me. Her tone of speech had the new intimacy that she had begun using with me as our circle became smaller, as everyone she met now said good-bye to her, knowing that soon we would disappear from their address books, invitation

lists, and memory; she turned toward me as the one who would ac-
company her into the unknown, her fellow *caminante* on her way
to *el destino*. Yet as much as I enjoyed being treated like an adult, it
was not a totally fair deal. I was expected to listen to my mother's
secret fears and to empathize with her anxieties; while on the other
hand, I could never reveal my most intimate thoughts to her—she
would be scandalized if she knew how much I had really given up
in the last year. I understood that I was to be an adult only when
she needed me to be one for her.

"It helps Mili to have something to do that she likes." I
smoothed out the wrinkled sheet of drawing paper that we had
found under Mili's bed as we packed her belongings. Tía Divina
had asked to take Mili to the beach while we worked. Mili had become agitated at the thought of being separated from us, but she
calmed down when she realized that it would just be her and Tía
going. She had a new problem now: she was afraid of crowds, covering her ears as if anything other than one person talking was too
much for her to bear. She said her head was noisy. She complained
of headaches and hid under beds and in closets. She had also taken
to wandering from the yard, but Mami had noticed in time for me
to run after her before she reached the end of our street. Her rest-
lessness was more frightening than her trances. Mami and I took
turns watching out for Mili, making sure she stayed busy and didn't
get too upset. This meant keeping the TV and radio off or the volume turned way down, and speaking in whispers. We looked for
ways to help each other and her, but we were distracted by our own
fears about the future, and I was exhausted from my duties as my
sister's keeper. I was not always patient with her. I had even lost my
temper a couple of times and yelled at her, told her that she belonged in an asylum.

"Consuelo, when you yell like this my head hurts. What is an
asylum?" Mili had gotten stuck on the word *asilo* that day, saying

"*Asilo*, Consuelo, *asilo*, *asilo*, Consuelo, Consuelo," over and over until I could not take it and had to run out of the house locking her in by herself. I did not go far, just a few times around the block, but when I returned she was under the bed sobbing. I had not told my mother, who had gone out for groceries that afternoon. But I knew then that I could not tolerate this kind of life for much longer. Mili did need to be somewhere where she could get the kind of help she needed. And I needed to have a life of my own outside *la familia*.

During this hard time the whole family tried to be kind and helpful to us: Tío Yayo had toned down his sermons and my aunts, grandparents, and cousins were treating us with deliberate tenderness, as people do when they are preparing to say good-bye. Papi was working his last days at the hotel, and Mami had relaxed her vigilance of him. She had turned regal in her pain, graciously accepting the roses on her way to purgatory. If Mili had a good day, Mami would smile and say Mili was improving, as if her daughter had the flu and would soon be completely well.

"Your sister does seem better, doesn't she?"

It was my job to answer the unanswerable questions now tagged to most of my mother's statements.

"Yes, she seems calmer, *más tranquila*, today," I answered each time she asked. It was a lie she needed to hear. I could see the panic in her eyes, and I knew I had the power to help her or to hurt her. So I spoke the words she wanted to hear: "Yes, Mili is doing better, Mami." I did not tell her that I was the one growing less calm, more impatient to change my life.

While packing, I had come across Mili's baby album and was sitting on the floor going through it. Mami had kept an album to give to each of us after we married. She had once said that as we got older we would find the photographs of our childhood more and more important, especially when we shared them with our children. I looked at Mili in her christening dress. She had been a beautiful baby, already smiling for the camera even though she was just a lace-wrapped little bundle in my mother's arms. María Milagros had seemed a perfect name, I had heard my mother say, since this happy baby had been such a miracle—so perfect and beautiful. It seemed that I was holding her hand in every picture, even when I was off camera.

I marveled at how in those early photos we were a nearly normal Puerto Rican family, our worst problems comparable to any other family's. Too bad we didn't have the right script; it could have been the cuento with the happy ending. But we missed cues, forgot our lines, got out of character, and lost our motivation. Whatever went wrong, it all changed, changed forever in a matter of a few years. We were now different people, no longer acceptably unhappy, but truly victims of *el destino*, case studies for what was soon to come—*la tragedia*.

All that time I had been using my letters to Patricio as a secret journal, a place to practice the language of my flying lessons, the vocabulary of escape. I had been sending my words in two languages into the widening void between us with no fear that my secrets would be betrayed. I told Patricio how my cousin, Miguel, had lectured me about "*la decencia*" even as he tried to seduce me. I told him how at school I was no longer looked at in the same way. The currents of gossip had shifted toward others whose scandals were more recent. Wilhelm's father had decided to move the family to California, where he was hoping to retire from the army. Wilhelm, like Miguel, seemed a bit scared of my new self: the new Consuelo who walked with her head up and an enigmatic smile that said *None of you knows who I really am. Nadie. Nadie.*

But maybe one person did know, the least likely of them all, Señorita Vélez. Our trip to La Perla had been her farewell gift, an image to take with me to the other side, in case I ever fell into the chasm of romantic remembrance of our island; what she had given me was either a pearl wrapped in soiled butcher's paper or a piece of dung in a velvet box.

I told Patricio that I felt I was growing up too fast, as he had done, maturing too early like the bananas in his old backyard that turned black and fell on the ground to be consumed by flies, rotting before reaching ripeness. I told him I loved him because he had given me tenderness and not asked for anything in return. I said I wanted to live with him as brother and sister.

Patricio wrote back to tell me that he was soon leaving the country on a buying trip to Europe. He and the famous designer would be traveling together for months. I should write to him at the old address; he would let me know when he returned. Patricio did not refer to my outpouring of fear and shame, my plea for his support, but he did add a postscript to his last letter.

You may leave the island, niña, but it will never leave you. We all carry the plantain stain with us, *la mancha*, inside or out, wherever we go.

I tried to visualize Patricio in the Old World, in the castles and rooms filled with gilded, ornate furniture and rich tapestries that I imagined Europe to be, and it wasn't hard. He had always decorated his life like a stage play. And he was happiest when he walked in the cobblestone streets of Old San Juan under its hanging balconies and fancy grillwork where he could imagine dramas being enacted in times past. I tried to envision him now as a grown man, but all I could see was my cousin's sweet boy's face as he held up one of his puppets or fed the chameleons.

I had been changed outside as well as inside by secrets, by private shame, and by the hard, hard days of the past four years. What had I become? I was still naïve enough to look for an answer in the mirror. I smiled as brightly as I could manage, tilted my head at different angles, but the image remained the same: I saw a thin girl, almost a woman, hair pulled back from a face that could have used a little makeup; the pallor of a recluse, the eyes lacking sparkle—or at least that's what Tía Divina had said. Mami had shrugged and sighed sadly. How could she be expected to care about the absence of dreams behind the eyes of her older daughter when there was such travail in her own life? I could see for myself what my aunt saw: how I had changed, was still being transformed by time and circumstance. But unlike the chameleon Lucila, a smile, a shift of posture, would not, could not, take me back to where I was when I had built palaces of glass in Patricio's backyard.

There were satellites in the night sky over Puerto Rico that year. On several occasions I accompanied Papi out to the beach at night to try to spot *Sputnik*, the "space ship" my father wanted to, needed to, see. He peered for hours through a hand-held telescope like the Lord Admiral of the Seas hoping for a glimpse of the Indies.

One time he was certain he had spotted *Sputnik* crossing the night sky over San Juan, another portent of the exciting future that awaited us in the New World, when all problems would be solved.

"Hija," Papi had whispered to me, as if we would scare the vision away by talking about it. He had put his arm around my shoulders, directing my gaze up to the sky. "Look." He handed me the telescope and directed my eyes to a spot so far over our heads that I nearly fell back into his arms. I looked and looked through my father's glass, but all I saw were the same stars I had always seen in our sky. The only difference was they were a little closer.

Tía Divina had packed her black Buick sedan with a picnic basket of Mili's favorite food: *pasteles* made from sweet plantains that Abuela had sent wrapped in banana leaves and tied with lengths of pink string, my sister's favorite color. Abuelo had sent an illustrated book of birds of the Caribbean for Mili to copy, and Tía Awilda had made coconut candy. It was *la familia*'s farewell gift to us, a few hours of freedom from the vigil, the constant worry over Mili, and for my sister, a sunny day to remember during the *días americanos*, the gray American winter days that lay ahead.

Mami and I had settled into a peaceful lethargy that afternoon, working slowly, packing Mili's things at our leisure, looking at her baby pictures and remembering happier times. I was beginning to feel that perhaps it was a good thing; maybe we were closing the door on pain, preparing for a journey that might lead us toward wholeness again. That day we were performing a ritual of departure, a ceremony women have always officiated over, as I later understood, this handling of objects, the calling up of memories, the careful wrapping and packing of possessions chosen as necessary, the discarding of others not valuable enough to carry great distances into the future.

As if barriers had been broken on taboo subjects, my mother brought up Patricio's name that day for the first time since he and his father had left the island.

"It is a shame that your Tío Domingo has driven away his own son."

"Does he know where Patricio is?"

"He doesn't speak of him in his letters to your father anymore, but he knows that Patricio is somewhere in Nueva York. Your uncle is married to another woman now. She is pregnant. That is all he seems to care about, except money. Money has always been important to him. He is full of news about his apartment building in New Jersey, which he has filled with tenants."

"Is that where we're going to live, Mami?"

"Domingo has saved the basement apartment for us. He wants Carlos to be near the furnace and the boilers since that will be part of his job. Apparently, he also intends to make your father a partner, *someday*."

The way she said "someday" let me know that she doubted such a partnership would ever really come to pass. In our family, Tío Domingo was the acknowledged business genius; Papi was the one who was good with his hands, the mechanic who could fix almost anything.

And then, once more, the hand turned the kaleidoscope, the pieces fell into another pattern—and everything changed.

We had finished sealing the cartons marked "Mili's Room," when we heard an urgent knocking at our front door. It made us freeze in place: Mami kneeling, holding a record album in her hands that featured "Besame Mucho," Mili's favorite song, me sitting cross-legged on the floor with my sister's art supplies in my lap. There was another volley of knocking. This sound spoke its own coded language, and both of us leaped up and ran to throw open our front door. A policewoman stood there; two squad cars had pulled into our driveway and yard—radios crackling, engines running.

Waiting in the air, a drama was about to begin. My mother swayed and began making sounds of distress, not quite sobs, more like the noises you make when you wake up from a bad dream. I let the policewoman into our house and helped my mother to her rocker. The sounds of distress were louder now. I saw that Mami had covered her face with her hands. Then the policewoman placed her hands firmly on my shoulders and made me sit next to her on the sofa. "*Cálmate, cálmate, niña.* You have to be strong so you can help your mother." It was then I realized that the strangled sounds were coming from me.

And so it was that in one brief instant everything changed. Tía Divina's gaze had shifted for mere seconds from her niece—who had been singing to herself at the edge of the water—toward an American cruise ship that had appeared on the horizon. Our María Milagros vanished in the time it took for Tía Divina to look at the ship, perhaps to daydream of herself strolling its decks for a few delicious seconds, and then to pull her eyes and mind back to the shore, to resume the work of watching *la pobrecita niña.*

Not seeing Mili in the spot where she had been just a minute or two ago, nor anywhere in sight, my aunt had run up and down the beach, calling out for her, alerting other people. I had later imagined chaotic rows of footprints that ended at the edge of a hotel's privacy wall and rounded back to the spot where Mili and my aunt had picnicked. In my mind I counted these footsteps silently until the high tide erased them.

Others had joined Tía's frantic search. A group of young people who had been celebrating someone's engagement had gone into the surf, swum as far out as they could manage, but found nothing. There was no trace of my beautiful sister in her red bathing suit, the siren with long black hair falling down to her waist. Oh, people had noticed her, yes. They remembered the señorita with the voluptuous body and the sweet face of a little child. But no one had seen her walk into the water, or out to the road.

As the hours passed and we searched the beach ourselves, Mami gave herself over to a pain so deep and sharp that she fell on her knees as if she had been stabbed, then got on all fours like a wounded animal, shaking and whimpering. Then, no longer able to support her own weight, she laid her body down on the wet sand as if trying to make the earth swallow her. I walked as far as I could into the shifting blue water, going knee-deep into the translucent turquoise, then up to my neck in the purple blue. I put my head under the nearly black water of the Atlantic. I swam in ever-widening circles until I was completely disoriented. There is no way to know in moving water if you are looking at the same spot or not. It changes before your eyes, yet it is the same—water, sand, rocks, and seaweed. Under the gently rocking waves, I called my sister in words from her private language: *Mar azul, aguabuena, aguamala, azul, azul,* please return my sister. I also prayed to Changó, god of rain and thunder, Lucila's protector. Here at the edge of the sea, he was master. No use begging the Catholic saints. They had not answered our prayers for years.

So tired I could no longer fight the pull of the currents, I dragged myself back to the beach. On the warm sand, I curled up into a tight ball and watched the others with a growing sense of detachment. I turned my eyes way up inside my head as I had often watched Mili do, and I finally understood how you could turn yourself inside out. Inside I was screaming, tearing my hair by the roots until I bled, wishing myself unconscious; outside I used my head as a periscope, surveying the scene of my family's *tragedia,* watching it unfold like a film, recording an appropriate soundtrack—cello music, low and mournful—storing every detail in my brain for future reflection.

Papi and my uncle had joined the police in the frenzied search for Mili that lasted until night fell. A small police boat was making desultory circles out on the water. I watched that boat's flickering light make its futile rounds; never again would I be able to see a light in the distance and think of it as anything but the loss of hope. Light reversed its meaning for me that night, and I have always, since then, felt more comfortable in darkened rooms.

To our eternal dismay, Mili's body was never found.

It is only through the eyeglass of the future that we can hope to find a pattern to our lives. It was much later that I saw these events, culminating in my sister's disappearance, as a sort of prologue to the rest of my life. Books have taught me now how to look for order in chaos. The symbols, images, and metaphors that will unlock the themes are laid out by the author for the careful, perceptive reader to assemble into meaning. When you reach the last page of the final chapter, you can say, yes, it was always there—why didn't I see it? In a novel *el destino* is plot. You can miss it on first reading. It is the forgotten gun, the mislaid letter, the open flame, the path of motivation and circumstance the author has constructed for the characters to follow. These same elements set a life in motion too—image, symbol, complication, crisis, sometimes resolution, sometimes not—but to try to understand your story you have to read it backward, each scene examined from the end to the beginning for there to be any sense of narrative. The plot is the last thing you invent.

There is one big difference, though: the meaning of human actions and tragic events may never become clear, no matter how you shape your story.

My Puerto Rican cuento had a conclusion that I could have never predicted from the clues given to me at the beginning. I was a girl born to *gente decente*, neither rich nor poor, proud people, intelligent people, who loved me, though they did not, or perhaps could not, see me for who I became as a result of motivation and circumstance. Finally, I was no more like my mother than Mami was like Abuela, than Abuela was like Mamá Isadora. Yet we each carried all the others in our bodies and our minds. Did I mention genetics? Yes, they played a part in our cuento too. But I believe that language is more powerful than chemistry. You are what you hear, what you read. And how you remember words, how you tell a story to yourself, makes *you* up. You tell yourself as you live your life.

The guilt I felt at doing things my mother would have never done was a result of hearing *her* story, the story of Angélica. I had learned who she was by what I heard others say, what I heard her tell me. Now, she had lost the thread of her narrative. Grief over Mili had disconnected her from her life story, the cuento she told herself as she played the role of wife, homemaker, and mother. The book had fallen out of her hands and come apart, and the pages had been scattered by the wind.

The only recourse Mami had was to become like a child again within her family, to let Abuela take her back to her casa and nurse her while she gave herself over to a sorrow so profound that she could not see me, her other child. The women gathered around her in a protective circle. They told and retold old stories as if they were giving my mother back her old vocabulary. She had to learn how to be a strong woman again. I was not a part of this, I chose not to be part of this. I did not need to hear the old stories again.

And, for once, my mother did not ask for Consuelo.

Epilogue: ADIÓS, BORINQUÉN

They stored Mili's things in a shed behind Abuela's house. I kept only one thing of my sister's: a tiny pink plastic telescope with a photograph of the two of us in it. It had been a fad one year to get a favorite picture inserted into a plastic tube that could be used as a key chain; sweethearts exchanged them. Papi had had one made of us that he later discarded. Apparently Mili had saved it among the many bright objects she kept in a cigar box. The picture showed me as a skinny brown girl in my play clothes carrying a chubby toddler on my shoulders. We were both laughing, our mouths wide open in childish abandon, as if someone off camera had told us the funniest joke in the world.

I left the things Mami wanted for herself at her mother's house. I felt that she should decide what she needed to keep now. I gave away all of my trinkets and toys—except for a few objects I could not part with, dolls Patricio had made for me, a smooth stone I had fished out of the sea. Papi let me make all the decisions about house, furniture, clothes, and even money. He wandered the beach during the day, slept on the sand at night. His close friends, his *compañeros*, knew that this was his way of grieving and took turns keeping him company while he walked along the shore. Their wives sent him food and coffee. He came home only to shower late at night. In the morning I would find his sodden clothes on the bathroom floor, smelling of seawater and sweat. I washed and ironed them and set them out for him. I knew he was still hoping Mili would appear on the beach, and her papi would be there waiting to bring her home. I kept hoping that when the time came for us to leave, he would be ready.

A few days before we were to take Pan American flight 298 to New York, I had already packed everything we needed into three large suitcases and one box. I had placed Papi's guitar in its battered old carrying case alongside our suitcases. The box contained my small library and Papi's song sheets I had found deep in a chest of drawers that also held a packet of love letters he had exchanged with Mami. But he was not home when the *público* picked me up that morning for the trip to Abuela's house. I asked the driver to stop by the part of the public beach where I suspected he'd be. I saw my father's figure in the distance. His clothes seemed to be sopping wet, clinging to his body. He was barefoot, his head turned to the sea. Not far behind there was another man, one of the friends who was always with him. I called Papi and waved my arms, but he didn't respond. I thought about running to him, but I knew he was so grief-stricken from losing our Mili, so burdened by this terrible turn his *destino* had taken, that he had no room in his mind or heart for me. Not yet. So I let him go just as I had let my mother go.

At Abuela's house I said good-bye to Mami in her mother's bedroom, where I found her wrapped in a chenille robe, sitting in a rocking chair like an invalid, her hair being braided by Tía Divina, whose own guilt about Mili had become a penance: to serve my mother, to minister to her like Magdalene washing Christ's feet, paying in silence for her moment of *descuido* when she had precipitated a *tragedia* by her inattention—this was what she needed to do to save herself.

The women had a new resolve. They could not reverse the effects of our devastating *tragedia*, but they could try to save the one who had suffered the most damage: Mami. The women knew they had the power to heal her. But they had to close ranks, let her work out her pain in the family cell they could form with their bodies. It had worked for them before, this intensive care ward in a war zone, and it would again.

But not for me.

I had to find other ways to survive. And I had to leave La Casa de la Mamá Isadora and start my story again in a completely new place.

Abuela shook her head in dismay when she heard I intended to board with Tío Domingo for a while, until I knew what I wanted to do. "*Pero, hija . . .*" She could not think of anything to say to me. It was clear no words could stop me from leaving the island. And so the women who had said so much that was right and so much that was wrong, and who, for better or worse, had shaped me into the Consuelo I was that day, stayed silent while I said good-bye to my mother.

Because she looked so defeated and so fragile, I knelt in front of her and laid my head on her lap and felt her hands stroking my hair.

"Consuelo, *mi consuelo*," she said softly. She gave me her blessing and I rose to my feet.

After Abuela and my aunts had all given me *their* blessings in a chorus of *Dios te bendiga, hija*, I walked out into a nearly blinding day at summer's end. Yes, our parents had aptly named my sister and me: she had been their miracle, and I had tried, for as long as I could, to take care of her, to keep the miracle in our lives. I could have been *their* Consuelo forever, now that she was gone. After their grief abated, they would have called me back to their side, to take up my old role. But I no longer wanted the part I'd been assigned. I preferred, instead, to be a different character in their stories. I'd play the part of the one who walked away from their never-ending telling and retelling of *la tragedia*. Even though, by doing so, I knew I might end up becoming the character always offstage, the one who can be talked about and reinvented according to the demands of the tale or the motives of the teller, the one who is called *la fulana*.

On a rainy day soon after saying good-bye to my mother, I took the Pan Am airbus alone to the mainland. The last thing I saw at takeoff was a bit of green speckled earth, elegant as a jewel resting on blue velvet. Columbus had called the island "the nipple of the New World," because it was so lush and fertile, a vision so alluring that the Lord Admiral of the High Seas had used the language of seduction to record his first sighting of Borinquén in his captain's log.

I kept my eyes on my *isla* until a sheet of rain clouds covered it completely. Until there was nothing below or ahead but *mar azul y cielo azul*.

ACKNOWLEDGMENTS

I am grateful to my patient editor and friend, Melanie Kroupa; my agent, Liz Darhansoff; to Jane Pasanen; and to my friends who read this book in various stages: Hugh and Patricia Ruppersburg, Betty Jean Craige, and especially to my *compañera*, Lorraine Lopez. I want to say thank you to my *colegas*: Rafael Ocasio, Edna Acosta-Belén, Rima Benmayor, Eileen Schmidt, Ruth Glasser, Frances R. Aparicio, and others, whose work on Puerto Rico and Puerto Ricans in the United States has always fed my imagination. I am especially indebted to my wise and learned friend Elena Olazagasti-Segovia, who shared so generously her time and her knowledge of our island and of the Spanish language. My thanks also to my research assistants, who helped me obtain obscure books and articles, find bits of historical and anecdotal information, and in many other ways helped me get my story told: Phyllis Sanchez Gussler, Brad Edwards, and Billie Bennett; and *mil gracias* to Winter Elliott, for her always gracious acceptance of my *every* odd research request. *Gracias a todos.*

GLOSSARY

adiós good-bye

adivinanzas riddles

agua water

aguacero downpour

asilo asylum

Así son los hombres. That's the way men are.

ataques attacks, nervous breakdowns

a todos to everyone

autopista highway

aventuras adventures (with a sexual connotation)

Ay bendito. Blessed be.

azul blue

bacalaitos/bacalao salted cod or fried cod fritters

barrio neighborhood

batea a wooden bowl, used in Santería ceremonies, where
   thunderstones representing an African deity's power
   are kept

bebita   "little baby"; endearment

bien   well

boba   silly, stupid

bombas   bombs or balloons; also, a slang term for breasts. Refers as well to a call-and-response game, often bawdy, played to music at parties and dances.

caballero   gentleman

café con leche   coffee with milk

Cálmate.   Calm yourself.

caminante   traveler

campesinos   peasants, rural dwellers

carretera militar   military highway

casa   house

casas decentes   decent houses, upstanding (respectable) homes

cielo   sky

cine   movie theater

cisne   swan

clave   code; also, the rhythmic basis for salsa music

colador   strainer, sieve

compañeros   companions, buddies

Con Dios, María, José...   a prayer, "With God, Mary, and Joseph..."

conquistador   conqueror

consuelo   solace, comfort

coquí   a small frog native to Puerto Rico

cosa de mujeres   a female thing

cotorra puertorriqueña   Puerto Rican parrot

cuartel   barracks

cuento   story or tall tale

¿De acuerdo?   Agreed?

del diablo   of the devil

descuido   carelessness

desgraciado   unlucky, damned

días   days

¡Dios mío!   My God!

Dios te bendiga.   God bless you.

doña   courtesy title roughly equivalent to "Mrs."

dos segundos, nada más   no more than two seconds

el chisme   gossip

el deber de la mujer buena   a decent woman's obligation

el destino   destiny

el fulano/a   the outsider, the outcast

el mal olor   bad smell

el mundo   the world

el relajo   ruckus

el ron   rum

El Señor   Jesus Christ

el tío   uncle

¿Entienden?   Understand?

entonces   then

¡Entre!   Enter!

entrometida   busybody, meddlesome woman

escándalo   scandal

ese/a   that

espiritista   spiritualist

Está enamorada de ti.   He is in love with you.

Está perdido.   He is lost.

Estás loca.   You're crazy.

familia   family

farmacia   pharmacy

flores de muertos   flowers for the dead

garzas   seagulls

gente decente   decent folk, moral (respectable) people

gente educada   educated people

gorda   fat

gracias   thank you

Gracias a Dios.   Thanks to God.

gringa   a foreigner, specifically an American woman

guapo/a   handsome, beautiful

guarapos   sugarcane liquor, herbal remedies

guayabera   light cotton shirt

hábitos   habits worn by nuns, by penitents, and by believers
    seeking a special favor from God

hacienda   a sprawling ranch

hermana   sister

hija   daughter

historia   history

hombrecito   young (little) man

independentista   pro-independence party member

indios   Indians, indigenous Puerto Ricans

infraganti   caught red-handed

jamonas   spinsters

jíbaros   the term for rural Puerto Ricans, who have a distinct
    culture and accent

la caña   sugarcane

la decencia   decency

la fortaleza   the fort

la isla   the island

La Isla del Encanto   Puerto Rico, literally "the island of
    enchantment"

la mancha   literally "the stain," which marks the unsophisticated
    island person

la mártir   the martyr

la moda   the latest trend or fashion

la mula   the mule

la noche   night

la pura verdad   the pure truth, the whole truth

la religión   religion

la sufrida   the suffering woman, the martyr

la tragedia   tragedy

la traición   betrayal

la vida   life

La Virgen   the Virgin Mary

la zafra   the harvesting season for the crops

leyendas   legends

línea   line; in Puerto Rico it is also the vernacular expression for privately owned public transportation

loca   crazy

los americanos   Americans

los baños   the baths, specifically the natural thermal pools

los Estados Unidos   the United States

machito   little man

madrina   godmother

mahones   blue jeans

malas influencias   bad influences

malas lenguas   gossipers, literally "bad tongues"

malcriada   bad-mannered, rude

maldito   damned

Malditos sean.   May they be damned, or A curse on them.

mamita   endearment, literally "little mommy"

mano derecha   right hand, used in the sense of "You're my right-hand man"

mañana   tomorrow

mar   sea

más   more

más seria   more serious, reserved, dutiful

maví   a Puerto Rican soft drink

medio luto   half-mourning

mi amor   my love, my darling

milagros   miracles

Mira.   Look (verb).

moscas   flies

muchacho/a   boy/girl

mucho gusto   with pleasure

mucho ojo   to keep a close watch on, literally "much eyes"

mujercita   young woman

mujer decente   decent, respectable woman

mujeriego   womanizer

mulata   racially mixed person (usually black/white)

muy   very

Nadie, soy Nadie.   Nobody, I am Nobody.

negra   black female

nena   dear, darling girl

niña seria   serious girl

No hay.   There are none.

No sé.   I don't know.

novelas   novels

novio   boyfriend

ojos negros   black eyes

olla   pot, pan

orden   order

¡Oye!   Hey, there!

para la familia   for the family

pasteles   pastries; in Puerto Rico, specifically meat pies

patria   native land

pava   straw hat usually worn by country people, *"jíbaros"*

pelo bueno   good hair

penitente   penitent

pepita   pit of a fruit

perdido   lost

pero   but

pestañas   eyelashes

piel canela   cinnamon skin

piragüas   shaved ice and sweet syrup treats, snow cones

piropos   flattery

plenas   a type of popular dance music in Puerto Rico

pobrecita niña   poor girl

polilla   literally "termites"; used pejoratively to mean low-class
   people

por favor   please

primo/a   cousin

problema   problem

promesa   promise; also, sometimes, a ritual carried out by a
   believer in Catholic cultures in exchange for a favor from God

público   public; also, the public bus

pueblo   town

puertorriqueño/a   Puerto Rican

pues   then

pura azúcar   pure sugar

puta   bitch, prostitute

Qué guapo.   How handsome.

Qué linda.   How cute, or How pretty.

quenepa   a tropical fruit

¿Qué pasa?   What's up?

querida   dear, darling

quinceañera   a fifteen-year-old; also, the coming-of-age party for
   a girl when she turns fifteen

ranas   frogs

reinita   affectionate name for a small native bird

repostería   bakery; a selection of cakes and pastries

¿Sabes?   You know?

sacrificio   sacrifice

señora   Mrs.

señorita   Miss; also connotes virginity

serpientes   snakes

Se sacrificó por su familia.   She/He sacrificed for her/his family.

sí   yes

siesta   midday nap

sillones   rocking chairs

sinvergüenza   shameless

situación muy seria   a very serious situation

taller   workshop

telenovelas   soap operas

tener un hijo pato   to have a faggot son. *Pato* means "duck";
   used pejoratively, it can mean "faggot"

Tenía mujeres.   He had women.

trágico   tragic

tranquila   quiet, calm, good-natured

trapo   rag

triste   sad

tristeza   sorrow

turista   tourist

turrones   nougat candy

un desastre   a disaster

un hombre grande ya   already an adult

un mariquita también   a fag too

¡Ven!   Come!

verdad   the truth

volar   to fly

Yo tengo un novio.   I have a boyfriend.